Early Praise for
The Stars Would Curse Us

"The Stars Would Curse Us is a heart grippingly romantic story filled with fairytale like trials, beautiful friendships and so many kick your feet and giggle moments. With just the right amount of swoon, banter, page turning adventure and a cliffhanger that is not for the faint of heart, Stephanie and Valerie have crafted an outstanding debut." - M.A. Brown, author of The Songs That Beckon

"Faex! What a journey. I didn't want either story to end...and the last page... Torture!" - Elle Beaumont, author of Immortal Realms Trilogy

"Combs & Rivers perfectly blend together a high fantasy adventure and an ACOTAR meets Hunger Games style plot that had me on the edge of my seat the whole time." - Lou Wilham, author of Witches of Moondale

"The Stars Would Curse Us is a mesmerizing world, weaving a tapestry of slow-burning tension, perilous gambits, and a twist that leaves readers spellbound till the very end." - DeAnna Hill, author of The Heat of Seas

"This intriguing series starter just isn't what it seems. Beautiful, dangerous, and a commentary of all things too real, The Stars Would Curse Us embraces femininity, the woes of naivety, and the exploration of a realm under the hand of oppression." - Shar Khan, author of Maiden of the Hollow Path

THE STARS COULDNT BREAK US

Book 1.5 - A Novella

Stephanie Combs
& Valerie Rivers

Midnight Tide
PUBLISHING

Published by Midnight Tide Publishing
www.midnighttidepublishing.com

Cover illustrations and design by Valerie Rivers
Character art by Valerie Rivers
Map based on original fantasy map illustration by Gustavo L. Schmitt
with adaptations by Valerie Rivers

Interior formatting by Stephanie Combs

Developmental/Copy/Line Editor - Rachel Bunner
Email: rachels.top.edits@gmail.com
Instagram: @rachels.top.edits

1st edition 2024

Paperback ISBN: 978-1-958673-94-2

Hardcover ISBN: 978-1-958673-95-9

Content Note

This story contains content that could be sensitive for some readers. There are scenes/mentions of violence, blood, animal mistreatment, pregnancy, a sick baby, and postpartum depression. There is also mild (non-graphic) sexual content.

If you have specific questions about any of these, or any you do not see listed here, please reach out to us at silverflamebooksllc@gmail.com

Important Note to Readers:

If you have not read Book 1 in The Stars Would Curse Us series, **STOP** reading now and begin with that story. This novella contains major spoilers for Book 1 and should not be read until you have finished *The Stars Would Curse Us*.

Pronunciation Guide

Characters

Arianwen - Ah-ree-AHN-wen
Verus - VAIR-us
Aella - AY-luh

Elemental Fae Races

Argenti - Ar-JEN-tee - water elementals/silver skin
Aurum - OR-um - fire elementals/gold skin
Aereus - AIR-ee-us - earth elementals/bronze skin
Adamas - Uh-DOM-us - air elementals/opalescent ivory skin

Places

Esterra - Eh-STAIR-uh
Iveria - Eye-VEER-ee-uh
Prisma - PRIZ-muh
Zephyria - Zeh-FEAR-ee-uh
Ilithania - IL-ih-THEY-nee-uh
Easthen Forest - EAS-then Forest

THE COURT OF WATER
NORTHEN IVERIA
LAKEHAVEN
WESTHEN ISLES
THE HOSPITIUM
SACRED LAGOON
IVERIA
THE BAKERY
HOME
THE COVE
BELOW MARKET
SOUTHEN IVERIA

Dedication

*To anyone who's ever had a broken heart, may
you find courage to love again.*

*...and to anyone willing to fall in love with a
papa goose cinnamon roll.*

RECAP

The Stars Would Curse Us

Arianwen, having slipped through the first marriage draft of the season, was preparing herself for an arranged marriage to Verus, a male she had never met. But it appeared fate had another path in store as she stumbled upon Wynn, a handsome wounded stranger, who had impossibly fallen from the sky. She risked all to heal his fatal wounds and journey with him to a hidden kingdom among the clouds.

As they traveled together to Zephyria, Wynn's true identity as the prince of the lost Court of Air was revealed. Their friendship blossomed, but an intense attraction sparked between them as well, and Arianwen began finding more reasons to stay than return home. Arianwen's worldview changed as she witnessed firsthand the atrocities of the ruling Iris while healing injured refugees and uncovering shocking truths about their rulers' origins and sinister intentions. A secret prophecy that spoke of one marked by the stars who would be the Iris' downfall was also revealed.

No longer willing to sit back and do nothing while knowing the truth of the Iris, Arianwen accompanied Wynn and his cabala on a rescue mission to Ilithania, where she nearly fell into the clutches of the Iris guards. Their perilous but successful journey brought Wynn and Arianwen closer together, leading them to finally give in to their growing feelings and attraction.

Despite finding freedom, purpose, and friendship in Zephyria—as well as a fledgling love—Arianwen continued to waver between listening to her heart and staying, or returning home to her family and duty. However, her new life crumbled when she discovered a devastating truth: Wynn was betrothed. Refusing to stay as his mistress, she gathered her strength and fled into the night, leaving everything behind.

I'VE GOT YOU

PROLOGUE

VERUS

Her name rang out across the packed courtyard, and I gasped as any hope I'd had left guttered out—a flickering flame doused by a wayward spray of water. Something cracked within me. I had begun to believe the stars might have been on my side with my betrothed's disappearance, and yet they'd failed me. Only three had been chosen out of thousands, but they'd called *her* name.

Clenching my fists at my sides, it took every ounce of willpower to stop myself from running to her. The muscles in my neck stretched tight as I watched her make her way to the front where the Iris Guardian stood. A sudden rage came over me, and the idea of tearing his neck from his body brought me a thrill. I'd have given anything to spare her from her fate. The Iris were a plague on our shores, and I felt powerless.

There was absolutely nothing I could do to spare the love of my life from being sent off to compete for one of them. Even if she did not win the hand of whichever Iris noble was next in line to be wed, she would never return to me.

"Calm yourself, Verus," my best friend, Tal, hissed next to me. "The last thing you need is to be taken off to the brig for insubordination."

"I won't even get to say goodbye," I gritted out.

"I know," he said, then cursed under his breath. "There's nothing you can do. She would never forgive you if you got yourself killed over this."

I sought her out, hoping she would turn around and I could look into her eyes one last time. "Please," I prayed under my breath. "Give me that at least."

The Iris guards escorted her toward the waiting ship, and my heart sank further. If only my parents had allowed us to marry, this never would have happened. But no, they needed me to marry above my station to help them. How would I ever forgive them for this?

At the last moment, she turned her head and her emerald eyes met mine. Pain and acceptance filtered through them, a silent message filled with love breaking through. I reached a hand toward her, as if I could touch her despite the crowd of Argenti that separated us. A single tear rolled down her cheek before she turned away, and I watched her walk out of my life forever.

CHAPTER 1
WEDDING DAY

ARIANWEN

This was always supposed to happen. The stars had charted this path for me. My arms wrapped around my middle as I tried to keep myself from heaving up my breakfast. The beading of my dress dug into my bare forearms as I took deep breaths, trying to ground myself.

Not a month ago, I had been dreaming of a life with *him*. I had convinced myself I could have a life and love of *my* choosing. This wasn't supposed to happen. Squeezing my eyes closed in an attempt to stop tears from ruining my makeup, I tried to calm myself.

In through the nose and out through the mouth. I practiced the breathing techniques Pluvia had shown me during my early days in Zephyria. *In for four seconds, hold, then out for six seconds.*

"Ari, you look amazing!" Leilani, my younger sister, exclaimed as she threw her arms around me. The nerves I'd been striving to keep at bay flooded back with even more intensity at the interruption. Feigning a smile, I half-heartedly hugged her back.

"Thanks, Lani. Mother outdid herself."

Leilani leaned back, brushing a stray curl from my cheek. "You know, she never stopped working on it, even when you didn't return home when you were supposed to."

My chest tightened. "As if she hasn't reminded me every day since I returned."

"Are you ever going to tell us what actually happened to you? I haven't seen you this depressed since our school days." Lani twisted a lock of her dark, wavy hair around a finger as her deep blue eyes met mine.

"Here I thought I was hiding it so well." I deadpanned. "I *really* wish I could say more, but I just can't." My mind immediately went to the star-shaped scar on my palm.

To the depths with him and his stars-damned oath.

"Well, I'm so glad you're home, even if you won't tell me anything. Now cheer up. You're getting married today, and you'll scare the poor male off with that frown on your face," she teased.

"You're absolutely right, Lani. Stars forbid I make a bad impression on the strange male I am about to spend my entire life with."

If the scandal surrounding my disappearance hasn't turned him away, I doubt a frown will.

I smoothed my hands down the front of my gown. It truly was lovely. The neckline plunged into a deep V, and the bodice hugged my curves while tiny, shimmering beads of coral and seashells created an intricate seascape of swirling blues and greens. The dress flared out below my knees, falling in soft waves around my bare feet. A macrame cape with lacelike webbing of cream-colored, hand-knotted seawool hugged my shoulders. Its long, fine tassels, which faded to a vibrant teal color, swept the floor behind me.

"Ari, try to be happy," Lani said, interrupting my perusal of my dress. "At least he's not Iris. Mother and Father made their arranged marriage work, I'm sure you can too. It's not as if you need to be in love with him." She fussed with a loose curl that kept freeing itself from the exquisitely crafted half-crown braid that delicately anchored the front of my hair while the remainder cascaded in voluminous waves down my back.

It took all the strength I had in my entire body to not break. Love. What I had always dreamed of and thought had been within my grasp. What a foolish desire.

Stars willing, Verus is someone I can respect, because that is all I can offer him. I will never love again.

I was a little nervous about living below—but my father was convinced that Verus would be able to move us above within the year. Verus had been showing much promise at the shipyard, which was the only reason my parents had agreed to the match originally. Stars only knew if anyone else would have been willing to marry me after my disappearance—I should be grateful that Verus and his family hadn't backed out.

Leilani pinched some color into my cheeks before grasping my hands in hers. "Big sister, I know you like to be the strong one for all of us, but you can rely on us too. Whatever great pain is in your heart, it will heal with time. I will come whenever you need me, and you know Kai and Aeron will put Verus in his place if he so much as looks at you funny."

I leaned forward so our foreheads touched, and my lips twitched into a grin. "Little sister, when did you become so wise?"

Leilani scoffed, "I've *always* been wise. You were just too stuck in your books and healing studies to notice."

Our shoulders shook with mirth, and I was incredibly grateful her presence had managed to soothe some of my nerves. She was only a year and half younger than me and my closest friend. Everything was going to be all right. Eventually.

Despite everything, I truly was glad to be home and surrounded by my family. The fact that I had considered not returning made me feel incredibly guilty. Iveria was home, and I would find happiness here. Zephyria had been a dream, the memories fading more every day.

My mind drifted back to that fateful night. Luminara had flown me to the border of the Court of Air, and I had made the rest of my journey home on foot. It had given me time to grieve and come up with a story to explain my prolonged absence. When I'd crashed through the door of my home, my mother had screamed and nearly fainted.

"We thought you were dead! Where in the stars have you been, Arianwen?" She collapsed onto the floor, her body shuddering with sobs.

I blinked, the memory so vivid, it could have been yesterday. She had vacillated between relief and anger, and I'd deserved every moment of her displeasure. Once the shock had worn off and a few days had passed, she had gone immediately into planning mode. Verus' family had agreed to honor the marriage arrangement in spite of my potential condition, and my mother had focused all her attention on making it a lavish affair.

Leilani and I made our way to the dock where my parents waited with the floating carriage that would take us to the sacred lagoon.

"It's about time you joined us," my father drawled. "I thought you might have run away again."

"Lev!" my mother reprimanded. "Arianwen did not run away—she already explained what happened. Today is a special day. Do not ruin this for me."

I glanced at my sister, and we both suppressed a laugh. How typical for our mother to make everything about herself on *my* wedding day.

"Yes, of course. I'm sure she didn't," my father said, giving me a pointed look.

He had not been nearly as dramatic as my mother upon my return. After kissing the top of my head, he'd said that he was happy I was back. His sharp eyes had drifted to the scar on my hand, and he'd given me a wary glance. I was just grateful he hadn't asked any questions, but I knew that he didn't quite believe my story. On the other hand, my mother had seemed to take personal offense at my inability to answer all of her questions. A fault which I felt like I'd be spending the rest of my life atoning for.

"Malakai and Aeron are already at the lagoon. Come now. Make haste. We mustn't keep everyone waiting," my mother said as she waved us into the modest carriage.

We raced toward the sacred lagoon with sea spray dusting our cheeks and salt-scented wind rustling through our hair. The closer we got, the more my nerves started creeping up on me again. My heart pounded in my chest as I gripped Leilani's hand. Closing my eyes, I started counting my breaths.

In, two, three, four. Hold. Out, two, three, four, five, six.

Once more, it took everything within me to restrain my tears as we sped off toward my stars-chosen future.

The sun was making its final descent as we arrived at the sacred lagoon, casting its golden light over the sand. My dawning ceremony hadn't been that long ago, and now I was returning to marry a male I had yet to lay eyes on.

My friends and family stood gathered to one side of the beach while a group of strangers, who I presumed to be Verus' friends and family, were gathered on the other. My parents led the way, followed by my sister and brothers.

Drums marked my arrival, accompanied by whoops and trilling howls of celebration. As I stepped onto the sand, the vibration of the drums hummed through me. I slowly made my way up the shore toward the large gathering while the long tassels of my cape fluttered behind me, caught on a slight breeze. Salt and sea filled my nose alongside the perfume of the tropical plumeria blossoms scattered abundantly on the sand. A large male stood facing away from me under an arbor of silver driftwood and luscious blooms. My breath hitched.

There was no turning back now.

CHAPTER 2

TRY TO BE PLEASANT

ARIANWEN

The drums stopped. A hauntingly beautiful melody floated around me, causing my skin to pebble in anticipation. The conch shells' airy tones mixed with the chorus of voices would be a sound I'd never forget. Time seemed to stop as Verus turned around to face me.

The first thing I noticed were his eyes. He blinked them as if in surprise before they shuttered, locking me out. They were the same color as the aqua water in the lagoon, but instead of exuding warmth, they evoked a sense of cool indifference, and part of me wanted to laugh. I understood what he was saying so subtly with his eyes: he wanted to be here just as much as I did. And how could I blame him after my disappearing act?

His broad shoulders and chest stretched the fabric of his dress tunic. The top had been left unbuttoned in an irreverent manner, platinum swirls of tattoos peeking through. His dark silver skin glimmered in the waning sunlight, and his thick, obsidian hair was twisted into a casual knot behind his head. As if calling me out on my perusal, his jaw clenched tightly and he looked away. Suddenly, I remembered that I was supposed to continue toward him, so I took a step.

His slight rejection and annoyance left me simultaneously embarrassed and angry. While I wanted to roll my eyes at him, I tried to paste a pleasant smile on my face instead, a faint blush coloring my cheeks.

Stars forbid I make him wait for this marriage we both so clearly desire.

I dropped my gaze as I followed the music, the drums coming back in as I made my way closer and closer. The silky flower petals cushioned the bottoms of my bare feet, and I tried to center myself once again as I walked toward the male I was going to marry.

My family and friends formed a semi-circle around me as Verus' family completed the circle on the other side. With each step toward Verus, the circle tightened until they surrounded us, fanning out from the canopy in waves. No longer two sides representing two families, but a mingling of both, to represent the joining of our lives.

When I reached him, I looked up once again and he tilted his head, a challenge in his eyes. Nervously accepting his outstretched hand, I stepped up to his side. He was so incredibly tall, my head barely reached his shoulder. His hand was rough with callouses and strong as he gripped mine.

The rest of the ceremony went by in such a blur, I could barely process the sacred vows tying us together. My nerves had fled and been replaced with a feeling of numbness. The first words I heard him speak were his promises to care for and cherish me. How could he promise that when we had never spoken a word before this? How had my parents gone through with it? How did anyone?

Suddenly, there was applause and shouting as a wave swept in from the sea. I gasped as the glowing water swirled around our feet, cinching us closer together, anointing us with its blessing. For just the briefest of moments, I thought everything was going to be all right as my element sent a surge of strength through me.

The crowd erupted into whistles and cheers, and the air filled with expectation as Verus leaned forward and briefly brushed his lips against mine. The kiss to seal our union. My heart fluttered uncontrollably in my chest, and the surge of strength I'd felt dissipated, leaving me weak.

It wasn't supposed to be like this. Our first touch, our first kiss, all in front of friends, family, and strangers. *He* was a stranger. I held back a sob while plastering that fake smile on my face once again as I tried to look anywhere but at him.

"Arianwen?" Verus leaned down and quietly spoke into my ear, wrapping an arm around me in what surely appeared to be an affectionate gesture but really was to keep me from falling. "I've got you."

The water swept back into the sea, children chasing after it, joyously splashing in its wake. Verus led me through the throng of our friends and family as they sang congratulations. His arm kept me steady as I attempted to smile and nod through it all. A sumptuous feast of fruit and fresh fish had been laid out, and he guided me to the settee and table that had been set for us.

"Can I get you anything? A drink?" he asked, his voice dripping with boredom and annoyance as I extricated myself from his arm and sat down.

What in the stars is up with this male? One moment, he is being kind and keeping me from falling, and the next, it's as if he can't get away from me fast enough.

"Some water would be wonderful, thank you," I said meekly, donning the mask of the submissive, obedient wife I assumed he expected.

Raising an eyebrow at me, he nodded before walking off to find me a drink.

The sun had almost dipped beyond the horizon, the lagoon lit up in the final rays of evening light. There was no going back, and a core part of me grieved my sudden loss of freedom. Not that I had ever truly been free.

Verus returned with my water and a nautilus shell of sparkling wine.

"Here you go, *wife*," he said somewhat sarcastically as he handed it over.

"Thank you, *husband*," I replied. The word sounded strange coming from my lips.

He sat down next to me, his large frame taking up the majority of the settee. As much as I tried to move over, there was simply not enough room to stop our legs from touching in the small space.

"Am I taking up too much space?" Verus asked, throwing an arm across the back of the settee and, looking far too comfortable with my obvious discomfort.

Sitting on the edge to avoid touching him more than I had to, I gulped the water down quickly before placing the vessel onto the table. "It's fine," I gritted out. "We *will* need to get used to each other eventually."

Verus scoffed, "Don't do anything on my account. Let's just get through this *celebration* and worry about the rest later."

I turned to glare at him. "Can you at least try to be pleasant? Our families put a lot of time, money, and effort into making this evening special."

He snorted then suddenly leaned toward me, encroaching on my personal space even more. "How pleasant do I need to be, *wife?*" His breath fanned against my lips, and I cursed my body's response to him. If I moved forward an inch, our lips would have touched.

Why does he have to be so stars-damned good-looking?

"I'm sorry! Am I interrupting?" My sister's voice broke me out of the spell Verus had cast over me. She gave me a knowing grin. "Please go back to whatever it was you were about to do," she teased. "I can come back later."

"No!" I cried out quickly, pushing Verus away. "We were just talking. Nothing to interrupt."

Lani stepped back, crossing her arms, the look on her face speaking volumes.

Verus suddenly dragged me onto his lap, wrapping an arm around my middle.

"What are you doing?" I hissed under my breath while trying to smile at Lani.

Verus leaned forward and lowered his face to my level, our cheeks touching. "Just being *pleasant,* wife." His words rumbled, causing unwanted shivers to course through me.

"Did you need something, Lani?" I asked, trying to ignore the overwhelming proximity of my husband, grateful when he leaned back, loosening his hold around me.

"I'm here to offer my congratulations, obviously," Lani crooned. "Along with my best wishes for a happy marriage. It appears you are getting along quite nicely."

My whole body tensed up as Verus' free hand traced a line down my arm. "Thank you. Verus has been nothing but . . . pleasant," I ground out.

Two can play at this game.

I moved my hand to Verus' thigh and squeezed, feeling him tense up behind me.

Stars, he's nothing but pure muscle.

Lani laughed brightly before wriggling her fingers in the semblance of a goodbye as she whirled and ran off to join some of her friends. The minute she turned, Verus picked me up and unceremoniously plopped me next to him as he moved uncomfortably on the settee.

"Already tired of being pleasant, *husband?*" I drawled.

"This marriage is a farce like most marriages in Iveria. If it weren't for the Iris laws, this would have never been arranged. The sooner you get it in your head that this is purely for convenience and will never be anything else, the better," he finished, not even giving me the courtesy of eye contact as he stared out at the revelers with boredom.

"You speak as if I want this," I replied. "Nothing could be further from the truth. You're just as insufferable as I thought you'd be."

I jumped to my feet, needing to get away from this male I was forever tied to, but my foot caught in my dress, and I started to fall. Before I could cry out, Verus lurched out of the seat and caught me. He helped steady me back onto my feet, and I stared up at him in disbelief.

"What? You thought I'd let you fall," he stated more than asked.

"I don't know," I mumbled as I straightened, making sure my dress was no longer tangled up with my feet. "Thanks . . ."

"You're welcome . . . This doesn't mean I suddenly like you."

"Stars, what a shame," I said drolly.

With my head raised high, I turned and marched off toward my family's tent. I was ready to get out of this dress.

Arrogant male.

My stomach grumbled as I passed by tables laden with savory meats and an array of fruits and vegetables. I stuffed a juicy-looking piece of fruit into my mouth, unable to stop the moan as it burst on my tongue, tantalizing my tastebuds with its flavor. The rush of sugar gave me a surge of strength, and I realized that being hungry was likely making me more irritable than I should have been. Perhaps I was being unreasonable toward Verus. Other than being a bit cold and distant, he truly hadn't done much to deserve all of my ire.

Grabbing a plate, I piled it high with a little bit of everything, knowing I would need my strength for the long night ahead. Argenti celebrations almost always went until dawn, and the night had just begun. Not wanting to head back and endure more of Verus' unpredictable behavior until my appetite was satiated, I nestled myself behind one of the large trees that surrounded the sacred lagoon.

I sighed as I leaned against it, looking up at the stars that had finally made their appearance. Glaring at them in silent judgment, I cursed under my breath. All of the emotions from the previous months threatened to overwhelm me.

How did I end up here?

Why would the stars have brought Wynn crashing into my life, teasing me with a glimpse of a better world, only to pull it so far out of my grasp that I felt as if I were drowning? Argenti couldn't drown, and yet I felt crushed under the pressure of expectations and disappointment. My chest felt tight, almost as if I couldn't breathe, and I fought back tears. I knew if I let them out, they would never stop.

In, two, three, four. Hold. Out, two, three, four, five, six.

Rolling my shoulders back, I straightened and looked down at my plate, my hunger mysteriously gone. As much as I would have loved to spend the remainder of the evening alone, I couldn't stay hidden for long—my family would start looking for me. The last thing we needed were more rumors about me disappearing from my wedding. I quickly shoveled the food into my mouth. If only it didn't taste like ash.

"Can you believe the Kalanis went through with this wedding?" I froze as the sound of my Aunt Rakhilit's voice cut through the night. My pointed ears perked up, but I decided to remain out of sight.

"It was such a shock," an unfamiliar female voice replied. "The entire scandal of her disappearance and return. I wonder what more her parents had to offer the Kalanis after she jilted their son. They would have been desperate to find a replacement so last-minute had the Kalanis backed out of the arrangement. Can you imagine?"

"I knew the Kalanis were desperate to move up in the Court of Water, but I didn't think anyone would be so desperate to allow their son to marry a disgraced female," my aunt said.

"You'd be surprised what people will do for a chance at a better life," the stranger added haughtily. "I am curious, though, how such a match came about in the first place. Why did your family agree to it *before* the scandal? Could it have anything to do with the bride's history with Lord Caelum?"

"Don't be ridiculous. It was only my brother's foolishness, thinking he could choose and mentor someone from below. I suppose it worked out for them in the end. But if it had been up to me, I'd have sent Arianwen away to live out her shame in one of the smaller villages. Why she even dared return and risk ill notice upon her family is beyond my comprehension."

My aunt's words caused my cheeks to burn with shame. A family member spewing such vitriol behind my back left me angry and hurt. I'd known my return would likely cause rumors to abound, but hearing the actual words cut through me like a knife.

"What surprised me most was how quickly they threw together the wedding celebration upon her mysterious return. Were they afraid of giving the Kalanis time to reconsider?" the stranger asked.

"We all know that there is only one reason they would rush this marriage," my aunt said.

"Do you think they bothered to inform the Kalanis of what they were getting into?" the stranger asked.

My aunt huffed indignantly. "Are you accusing my family of trickery? That is all rumor at best."

I rolled my eyes. Funny how my aunt was willing to speak harshly about me, but as soon as it might cause her to look bad, she was back on my side.

"No! Of course not," the other female said defensively. "I was merely suggesting that this could never become a love match if thrown together under false pretenses."

I squeezed my eyes shut. I'd had enough. Jumping to my feet, I rounded the tree, somewhat pleased when I saw my aunt's eyes widen in shock, a flicker of shame flashing over her face.

"Aunt Rakhilit, dearest, so nice to see you," I said, my voice saccharine.

"Ari, darling, you look lovely," she replied, quickly schooling her features. Her bracelets jingled as she clasped her hands together. "Congratulations on your marriage. I am ever so happy for you."

Liar.

"Thank you. I must be off to find my husband. I'll see you later," I quipped, pointedly ignoring the other female whose eyes held clear judgment.

I had no intention of finding my husband, but they didn't need to know that. Catching Leilani's eye from where she stood chatting with some friends, I nodded my head toward the family tent, a plea for help in my eyes. I was relieved when she smiled broadly and started heading in that direction.

Filling a shell with rainwater, I gulped it down, the refreshing liquid soothing my dry throat. The sound of joyful laughter and splashes drew my eyes to a group of younger fae who danced and frolicked about in the shallow waters, the algae lighting up with each crash of a wave or stomp of a foot. The harmony of the seaflutes and the beat of the drums pulsed through me as I stood watching, my lips tilting into a smile at the reckless abandon with which the younglings celebrated. Argenti knew how to throw a party, and dancing was in our blood. Almost unwillingly, I felt my hips begin swaying to the rhythm surrounding me. I could lose myself in it, and perhaps I should. Let tomorrow's troubles worry me in the morning, forget about the husband who wanted nothing to do with me.

A group of dancers, who were blissfully clapping and stomping to the music, beckoned me to join them. I danced and twirled, allowing myself to get lost. Weaving in and out of the circles of dancers, I let go and was free. The heavy pressure that rivaled the depths of the sea had finally lifted, and the evening flew by in a flurry of dancing and feasting.

"Ari, aren't you glad you came back? Verus is so handsome!" Leilani shouted as she dragged me into another dance, her face flushed and aglow.

I rolled my eyes at her while laughing as we twirled and stomped in a traditional dance, the tassels of my cape swinging around me like wings.

"What? You don't think so?" She quirked an eyebrow as she spun out and back in toward me.

"He's easy on the eyes, that's for sure," I admitted before clapping my hands to the rhythm as my hips swirled from side to side. The new dress she'd helped me change into was better for dancing. While still formfitting from the hips up, the lower half was made up of a skirt of fine tassels that would give me the freedom to swim and dance. I tested it out with a sequence of twirls, my right foot sending up a spray of sand as I stomped to the beat of the drums.

"He can't take his eyes off you, Ari."

I snorted. *Unlikely.*

We traded places, and I glanced over her shoulder. Surprisingly enough, Verus' eyes tracked our movement from where he sat at the table, making me self-conscious about the expanse of legs that peeked through the curtain of tassels as I danced. His hulking frame was sprawled out casually on the settee, a drink in hand as he laughed with his friends. He nodded with a wide grin that suggested their banter was less than virtuous.

Our eyes met, and he raised a thick, dark brow in acknowledgement. Unsure of how to respond, I flashed him an awkward smile before switching places with Leilani again.

Leilani's eyes suddenly sparkled as she looked over my shoulder.

"Lani, is he coming?" I asked, trying to keep my voice hushed even amid the spirited celebration.

She nodded excitedly. "It looks like his friends convinced him to finally get off his arse and join the party."

My heart started racing, and a slight panic set in. Dancing with him would be expected. I couldn't exactly continue ignoring him all evening, and perhaps he realized the same. Faex. Verus cleared his throat behind me.

"May I have this next dance, wife?"

CHAPTER 3

ONLY ONE SEAHORSE

ARIANWEN

I squeezed my eyes closed and took a breath before turning around and giving him a once-over. It was clearly paining him to be here asking for a dance, and suddenly, my panic fled. Away from his friends, he was just as uncomfortable as I was. Giving him a brief nod, I took his proffered hand.

It's just one dance. I can survive that. People will talk if we don't dance together at our own wedding.

The stars were clearly against us as the music slowed from the rousing beat to something more intimate. He grabbed my other hand in his and led me through the steps, our arms raised overhead as he drew me in closer and then we stepped apart. He turned me so that my back was to his front, and our bodies moved fluidly to the rhythm of the drums. He was a good dancer, I'd give him that.

"Are you enjoying yourself, wife?" His voice rumbled through me as he stepped closer.

"Our parents threw us a wonderful party."

He turned me again so we were facing each other. His height had my face directly in line with his chest, and I couldn't help but stare at the swirls of tattoos peeking through the opening of his shirt.

"See something you like?" he asked, pride coloring his tone.

I tilted my head back, meeting his gaze, my skin flushed from the dancing and embarrassment of being caught staring. "Oh, just admiring your tattoos and wondering how far they go."

Verus' lips twisted into a sardonic grin. "If you want to see, all you have to do is ask."

"I'm sure I'll see them eventually. I'm in no rush."

Verus rolled his eyes. "You wound me, wife."

"I didn't realize you had such a fragile ego, husband."

"Good to know you'll keep me on my toes."

He twirled me again, this time pulling me flush against his chest, his hands lowering to my hips. My traitorous body responded to his touch. He leaned down to speak into my ear, but I couldn't hear a word as the innocent motion reminded me too much of *him*.

Pushing off of Verus, I called over my shoulder as I moved away. "I'm sorry. I need to take a break and get something to drink. Thank you for the dance."

I couldn't look at him. I couldn't face him.

Why had he agreed to this marriage? Was this purely about status? Surely he could have found another female for the marriage requirement.

Hurrying back to our table, I picked up my water and poured it down my throat. Guilt racked me. I should have never gone through with this wedding. Maybe I should have tried to make my way back to Zephyria and lived in exile.

I squared my shoulders—I had made my choice and was going to have to live with it.

Dawn was nearly upon us when all the women in my family gathered around, layering me with blessings. My mother and father kissed my cheeks and said their goodbyes. I was nearly dead on my feet as Verus led me to the temporary floating dock and what I presumed was his floating carriage.

Before I could climb inside, Verus tutted, "That carriage is not mine, *my lady*." I looked up at him in confusion and watched as he untied the reins of a magnificent, blue seahorse that had emerged from the water beside it. Embarrassment tinged my cheeks pink as I realized my assumption had only served to hurt his ego.

He held out his hand, and I took it begrudgingly, only because everyone was watching. After easing me into the water and onto the large saddle, I clung to the beast's neck as Verus hopped on behind me. Not wanting to be seated in his lap, I tried to move forward and put space between us, but the seahorse had other ideas and reared back. With my back flush against Verus' muscular chest, I tried to ignore the way his warmth surrounded me.

"Why am I not surprised you haven't ridden one of these before," he scoffed quietly. "My apologies for not giving you a comfortable carriage to ride in." His tone dripped with bitterness, and I felt shame at my assumption once again. I didn't need a carriage. If only I could tell him about flying on aquilas and traveling across Esterra with no comforts, perhaps he would have held his tongue, but of course, my oath would not allow it. I wasn't the spoiled female he assumed me to be, at least I wasn't trying to be.

"Try to relax," he continued. "Let your body move with the seahorse or he'll send us flying. Let's not get bucked off and stranded this far from home."

"I don't think he likes me much," I retorted, though it struck me as odd, since most sea creatures loved me.

Verus wrapped his thick forearm around my waist, securing me to him. "Don't worry. I've got you."

A wave of nausea swept through me. I needed this night to be over. Being surrounded by his arms and his fresh, musky scent, hearing the cries and cheers of our family and friends as we left to supposedly start a life together, I couldn't take it.

"Please, just take me home," I said. With a fake smile pasted on my face, it took all of my strength to hold back tears as I waved at everyone. Within moments, we dipped below the water and I let them go, knowing the sea would sweep them away.

"We're home, wife. Let's get you to bed."

The words "home" and "bed" startled me awake more than they should have as I was brought back to reality. I couldn't believe I'd fallen asleep on the back of a seahorse—in his arms, no less. But I was eager to hop out of the saddle to put some distance between us.

We were no longer on the surface but down below, as Verus lived in one of the underwater homes in Iveria. The water was dark and chilly so deep, and I wrapped my arms around myself tightly as I waited for Verus to unsaddle and stable the seahorse in its designated stall. He patted the creature's nose, then tossed him a treat that the large beast sucked down its tapered snout. Verus took my hand in his strong, calloused one and swam us to the home above the stalls.

I followed Verus through the water barrier into a cramped, dry mudroom entrance that led directly into the kitchen. My gaze wandered around the small home, hoping to catch a glimpse into the stranger I was now married to. It was surprisingly cozy, given his cold and brusque personality.

"Well, this is it," Verus said somewhat gruffly. "I know it's not much, but I hope you will be comfortable here for now."

"This is lovely," I said, and I meant it, despite everything.

Verus led me down the short hallway to what I presumed was supposed to be our shared space. We passed a small bathing chamber and one other door, and I couldn't help but wonder what lay within. He opened the bedroom door, and I immediately spotted crates with some of my belongings stacked in a corner. They had been delivered throughout the previous week as I had packed everything from my family's home. Reality came crashing in. This truly was my home now. There was no turning back. But how was this going to work? How in the stars were we going to share a bed? A home? Our lives?

Verus walked over to a large wardrobe and opened it, revealing my clothes hanging neatly inside.

Breaking the awkward silence, Verus finally spoke again, his tone flat. "I put away some of your things for you." He paused as if unsure of what to say next. "I'm going to get ready for bed."

He grabbed a pair of pants and walked back out the door toward the small bathing room, and I immediately wrapped my arms around my middle, trying to remember to breathe. It wasn't supposed to be like this. Standing frozen next to the bed, I felt ill. I was utterly exhausted, and the faint notion that he might expect me to perform any wifely duties made me want to swim away and never come back. All I could do was hope that he had as little interest in me as I did in him.

Verus cleared his throat behind me, and I whirled. He was leaning against the door frame, a sliver of silver skin near his waist showing where his tunic was now untucked.

Stars, stop looking, Ari!

"Having trouble undressing, wife?" he drawled, his eyes glinting in the dim light of the lamps.

I flushed slightly. "Actually, would you mind unhooking the back of this dress? I don't think I can do it myself . . ."

His eyes flashed with something indecipherable, but he walked over to me, motioning for me to turn with his hand.

The dress was held together by tiny buttons that started just below my shoulder blades. I could feel Verus' breath on the back of my neck, and his scent drifted over me as his fingers deftly unbuttoned the dress. It started to loosen, and I crossed my arms in front of me to keep it from sliding off.

"Thank you. That should be good enough," I murmured quietly, a slight chill coursing down my spine as I felt the briefest sensation of fingers on my skin. Turning back to face him, I gathered my courage and finally asked, "Are we really going to do this? You clearly do not like me, and I don't like you. How is this going to work? What do you want—expect from me?"

His eyes darkened with annoyance. "You're right, *wife*." He marched over to the bed and grabbed one of the pillows. "I'll take the couch." He stalked back out of the room, the door shutting firmly behind him, leaving me with my mouth agape.

Had that really just happened? I should have been relieved, but instead, familiar feelings of being unwanted and unworthy crept in.

Faex. What in the depths is wrong with me?

I should have felt overjoyed that I didn't have to share a bed with that insufferable male, but instead, I felt . . . lost and alone.

Stepping out of my gown, I draped it over a small settee before putting on one of my nightgowns I found hanging in the wardrobe. Exhaustion came over me, and as much as I wanted to bathe and undo the braids and remove the shells and beads woven into my hair, I did not have the energy. I collapsed onto his bed and immediately drifted off to sleep, surrounded by the faint musk of sandalwood and the sea.

I awoke completely disoriented, unsure of the time or if it was even the same day anymore. Living under the sea meant the water outside my window might be a little brighter during the day, but not nearly enough to fully orient myself. Stretching my arms overhead, I caught a flash of color outside the window as a fish swam by. Would I ever get used to living below? I supposed I didn't really have a choice at this point.

The smoky scent of roasted vegetables tickled my sensitive nose, and my stomach grumbled. Food needed to happen as soon as possible. I got out of bed and threw on a robe, peeking my head out the bedroom door before hurrying to the small bathing chamber across the hall.

Delighted to find a basin of fresh water, I washed my face, taking time to unravel the giant mess of braids and tangles. Regardless of how hard I tried to tame them, my curls would not cooperate without a full bath, but my stomach had other ideas. Piling my hair into a loose knot on top of my head, I stared at my unpolished reflection. It wasn't as if I was trying to impress my dear husband after all. He might as well get used to me, messy hair and all.

Following my nose, I crept toward the kitchen only to find Verus standing over a fire in low-slung pants and no shirt, his muscled back on proud display. Stars. The tattoos I had seen on his chest wrapped around his shoulders and trailed down his back in intricate patterns. I couldn't help but wonder if they held any meaning to him.

"Good morning or afternoon or whatever time it is," I said, trying to sound pleasant as I walked in. "Without the light from the sun, I truly have no idea what time it is down here."

Verus snorted in response. "I'm sorry my home isn't closer to the surface for you, wife."

The derision in his tone bothered me. Did he really think I cared about any of that? Yes, it would take some adjusting, but I didn't think of living here as beneath me.

"Already in a mood, I see," I retorted. "I'm not complaining, just give me some time to get used to it down here."

I could see the tension in Verus' shoulders as he pulled something off the fire, refusing to even turn and look at me or respond.

Wanting to make peace with this male I was now married to, I said, "That smells delicious. How nice to know that you can cook."

Finally turning around to face me, he leaned against the counter and crossed his arms, his eyes perusing me from head to toe. "I've lived on my own for a few years now—it was a necessity."

"Good for you," I remarked, trying to keep my eyes on his face and not on his pectorals. "I'm not the best cook, but I'll do what I can."

"Don't bother," he replied. "I can take care of myself. I don't need you burning the stew."

I took a step back, trying not to take offense. "I never said I was terrible, but fine. If you want to handle that, I'll make myself useful in other ways."

His lips turned down. "Maybe I wasn't clear, but I don't need you to do anything for me."

I flinched at his tone. Even if that were true, I felt I had a role to fulfill as a wife, and by making me feel unnecessary . . . I couldn't quite explain why it bothered me so. Maybe I had been a fool to think we could figure out a way to live harmoniously.

The silence between us was palpable. He stared at me as if waiting for a response, but all the words I wanted to say had fled. Rolling his eyes, he straightened before turning back to the counter to serve himself some food. "Just stay out of my way, and I'll stay out of yours. Does that work for you?"

"Fine," I huffed. "Could you at least put on a shirt?" I didn't need the constant distraction.

He spun back around, a wicked smirk on his face. "Why? Does it bother you?"

"Obviously, or I wouldn't have said anything!"

"It's my house. I'll wear what I want."

"Fine!" I growled again, whirling and leaving the room. I needed to get away from him before I said something unforgivable. Loathsome, irritating, disgustingly handsome male. Why did he have to have the personality of an arse? Faex.

I stomped back to the bedroom, forcing myself not to slam the door in a completely childish manner. How was I going to live like this? I needed something of my own. I needed to get out of here and find a way to get back to my training as a healer, even if he didn't like it. Some concessions would need to be made between us. This was my house too. If he was going to insist on wearing hardly any clothes, I was going to make some of my own demands.

I quickly sifted through my belongings until I found just what I was looking for. After changing into something a little more *comfortable*, I spun back to the door, ready to lay my claim, but all my confidence fizzled out as soon as my hand reached the door handle. I threw myself onto the bed and curled up into a ball, hating that his scent surrounded me, only further reminding me of the male I was bound to.

CHAPTER 4
ONE CONDITION

ARIANWEN

Unable to resist the gnawing hunger any longer, I decided to risk bumping into my obnoxious husband. Thank the stars the kitchen was empty. I rummaged through the cupboards for servingware, settling for the first dish I could find—I'd have time to familiarize myself with the kitchen later. My impatient stomach had me standing at the counter, shoveling Verus' cooking into my mouth as quickly as I could. Damn the male, but he could make a fine dish.

Once the hunger pains had finally eased, I filled a large glass of water and drank my fill.

What I wouldn't give for some coffee right about now.

Damn Wynn for introducing me to that addictive treat and for the subtle ache I felt whenever he came to mind. There would be no more coffee in my future. It's not as if Iveria received exports from down south in Ilithania. It truly was a shame how the Iris kept us all separate. After all I had learned, it made sense. What easier way to oppress people and keep them from learning the truth than by separating everyone.

The house was still and quiet, making me wonder if Verus had left. Wanting to take advantage of his absence, I left the kitchen and turned the corner to check out the small family room I had only glimpsed earlier. I startled as I found him sitting wide-legged on a sofa, reading through a notebook with a steaming cup of tea in hand.

His eyes flicked up and widened. "What in the depths are you wearing?" he spat out.

"This is my house now too, right?" I replied with a smirk. "Surely, if you can be comfortable, so can I."

He growled in annoyance, and I couldn't help but chuckle at his discomfort and the slightly reddened tips of his ears.

"You've made your point, now go put something else on," he demanded.

I crossed my arms in front of me as he quickly looked back down at his notebook. My sister must have packed the flimsy nightgown for my wedding night. It barely covered my behind, and the neckline dipped into a deep V, showing off my assets.

"Listen, Verus, I know this situation—this marriage—is not ideal." I fumbled for the right words. "It's clearly not what either of us wanted. But can we try to find a way to get along?"

His eyes flicked back up toward mine, as if daring me to continue.

"Yes, I disappeared during my matri-ritus, and I'm sure you were informed of my current state, but you still agreed to this. Why?"

He set his drink down and stood suddenly, towering over me. "So it's true then." His eyes landed on my stomach.

"Yes," I gritted out. "Why in the stars would I lie about that?"

"Good," he replied simply, then brushed past me as he left the room.

What in the stars? I shook my head in confusion but decided not to let my fears get the better of me.

"Wait!" I called out. "I wasn't done." I reached the hallway and caught him stepping into the bedroom. While he didn't respond, he left the door open, so I took that as an invitation to enter after him.

I was greeted by the sight of him pulling a shirt over his head, his muscles flexing in a way that made me feel things I did not want to feel.

"I'm going to continue my training as a healer," I stated.

"All right."

"You said earlier you don't need me to cook for you, so as far as I'm concerned, we can share the responsibilities of keeping the home clean as well as all the cooking."

"And . . .?" he drawled.

"I'll wear appropriate clothing as long as you do the same," I continued as I reached for a robe and tightened it around myself. "At the very least, keep a shirt on."

He rolled his eyes and sighed. "You're asking for quite a bit there, wife."

"Well? Can we agree?"

He took a deep breath and looked up at the ceiling before finally returning his gaze to mine, his eyes serious. "Yes, I will agree to all—well, most—of those requests on one condition."

He took a step toward me, and I swallowed. Why was he so stars-damned tall? I tried to stand my ground and not cower as he took another step.

"What condition?" I asked.

With surprising gentleness, he reached down and placed one of his large palms on my stomach. "This is my child."

I reared back in shock and sputtered, "What? Why would you say that? Why would you do that? Don't you want to know how this happened? Who—" The mark of my star-sworn oath started burning, and I winced.

Verus tilted his head in confusion. "What's wrong? You look like you're in pain."

Surprised at his sudden care for my well-being, a strained laugh burst out of me. "A side effect of my *running away*, I suppose," I said, lifting my hand to show him the mark. "I'm unable to speak of where I've been or what I went through."

Verus stared at the mark, a dark look flitting over his face. For a moment, I thought he'd ask for more, but then he shrugged. "I won't ask you about your past, and you won't ask me about mine. Can we agree on that?"

While that seemed fair, a part of me didn't like agreeing to never knowing anything about his past. In my case, I literally couldn't say anything
about the previous few months, but agreeing to this meant living with a
stranger forever. Was I truly willing to do that?

"For now," I finally said. "I'll agree to that for now."

"Fine," he muttered. "Now, I am not spending the rest of the night on
that uncomfortable sofa, my neck is killing me. This is my room, and I'm
sleeping in my bed tonight."

"I'm sorry, what?" I questioned, taken aback at the sudden change of
subject. "Where am I supposed to sleep?"

He rolled his neck while squeezing it with the back of his hand. "My
bed is big enough for two. We can share tonight."

"You expect me to share a bed with you?" I asked, flabbergasted.

"What? It's not like anything is going to happen," he scoffed. "Isn't that
what married people do?"

I huffed a laugh. "You're unbelievable. I'd rather sleep on the floor than
sleep next to you."

"Fine with me." He leaned down, grabbed a pillow off the bed, and
threw it at me. My arms went up just in time to catch it before it hit me
in the face.

"You arse!" I cried.

His lips turned up into a devilish grin. "Better you find that out now
rather than later."

I resisted the strong urge to scream into the pillow. Clearly, we weren't
going to get anywhere like this. Pasting a saccharine smile on my face, I
walked toward the bed.

"You know what? I changed my mind. The floor actually sounds just a
bit worse than sleeping next to you, so I'll make do for one night."

Verus rolled his eyes. "Fine by me. Just keep to your side of the bed."
He fluffed another pillow and stripped off the shirt he'd just put on. I
quickly looked away, not wanting to get caught staring. "If you make

another comment about me keeping a shirt on, I'll take my pants off too," he said. "I prefer to sleep naked, but I'll keep them on just for you, *wife*."

My face turned bright red. "How thoughtful of you, *husband*," I sputtered awkwardly. He was obviously trying to get a rise out of me, but I wasn't going to let him. I placed my pillow on the other side of the bed before slipping my robe off and sliding in. Why sleeping next to him made me so nervous, I wasn't quite sure. Perhaps because he was actually my husband and this is what we were supposed to do? Or perhaps it was because he seemed to loathe the water I swam in. Either way, my feelings were all manner of confused.

"We can move your belongings to the other room tomorrow," Verus said gruffly. "There's no bed in there now, but we can get you one soon."

"Thanks," I replied.

Verus reached over and turned off the lamp, muttering a good night. As I lay submerged in the darkness, my mind couldn't stop thinking about our conversation and how our marriage would work. I should count it a blessing that he had so few questions about what had happened to me and how I'd come to be in this condition. Perhaps I should just thank the stars that he was willing to accept the child as his own and try to move forward, yet so many fears plagued my thoughts. What if the child were star-blessed with more than one power? What if they looked like their father instead of like me? Would we have to go into hiding? The last thing I wanted was for the child to be taken by the Iris. If only I hadn't rushed to leave Zephyria . . . maybe I could have made some kind of life for myself there on my own, even if it had been without *him*. But it was too late. What was done was done. It was no use looking back and wondering at a future that would never be.

I lay on my side, turned away from Verus, trying to make myself as small as possible. I took measured breaths in and out, allowing the close proximity of my element to help me feel safe even with the ornery male lying next to me.

CHAPTER 5

SLEEPLESS NIGHTS

VERUS

Stars help me. My wife was going to be the death of me. Her scent permeated the entire home, I couldn't escape it, and now we were sharing a bed. Torture, sheer torture. Sleep evaded me and was restless at best. I had no need of a wife, and if it weren't for the damned Iris, I would have been content to live the rest of my life alone. My heart had sailed off on a ship to Prisma, and nothing would bring it back.

This was supposed to be the home I built with my stars-chosen mate. Instead, I was sharing it with a stranger. My heart ached at the thought. We'd never said the claiming words, but I knew in the gaping hole where my heart had been that she had been mine.

I looked over at my sleeping wife. Her brow was furrowed, as if something were troubling her in her sleep. I'd been told she was beautiful, but she was nothing like I had expected. There was a familiar, weathered look in her eyes, like she'd given up much to be here.

Despite that, I could see determination and a sliver of hope seeping through the cracks, and a part of me hated it. It took strength and will-power to move forward even with the heartbreak that hung heavy in the air around her. I didn't like how it shone a light on my unwillingness to do so.

My eyes traced her sleeping form, the dips and curves of her body, the pouty lips ripe for kissing. She was a catch, and any other male would've considered me a lucky brute to have the privilege of being near her. My body had no problem with her—no, that wasn't the issue. A primal part of me was curious to fulfill our marital duties, but neither my heart nor my mind would allow it.

I had the feeling she wouldn't be game for something purely physical at this point anyway, or perhaps ever. Thank the stars for that, because I didn't need to add guilt to my running list of negative feelings. A wife deserved to be loved and cared for, which was more than I had to offer. As luck would have it, I was now partnered to a wife who had as little desire for a romantic marriage as I had, and it was best it stayed that way.

Better for her to loathe me. We could keep up appearances, but that's all this could ever be. If I hadn't known better, I'd have said the stars had fated this loveless match, because in its own twisted way, it seemed to be exactly what we both needed.

Arianwen shifted in her sleep, a delicate hand coming to land on my chest. My heart did a funny little thing, and for a moment, I debated whether or not to leave her hand there. I groaned and picked it up with my forefingers, dropping it back over onto her side of this suddenly too-small bed.

I had to remind myself that this was for my family back in the Westhen Isles of Iveria. They had put all their hopes on me to secure a better future for them. My apprenticeship with Arianwen's father and then the opportunity to marry his daughter had been a dream come true for them. I just never expected her to be so . . .

Arianwen rolled over in her sleep, the sheet slipping lower to expose more skin that her nightgown had already been doing a poor job of covering. I scrubbed my face in my hands. Curse the stars and their fickle ways.

Stretching my arms above my head, I couldn't hold back a yawn. Faex, I was exhausted, but chances were slim of me falling back to sleep.

Might as well get started on breakfast. But first, I need a cold bath.

"Good morning, husband," Arianwen said as she breezed into the kitchen and grabbed a plate. "What choices have we to eat today?"

"This isn't a restaurant, you know," I said grumpily. "You're lucky I made enough for the both of us."

"You made it clear my skills were not welcome in here," she snapped, her sunny demeanor quickly melting into storm clouds.

"Spinach with eggs," I grumbled.

"Sounds perfect," she replied before helping herself to a meager serving and making her way to sit down.

"Uh, wait," I stopped her, topping her plate off with a generous portion of spinach and the rest of the eggs, despite her minor protestations.

"Such a papa goose," I thought I heard her say under her breath. *What?* I shook my head as I poured myself another cup of strong tea. I was going to need it to make it through the day.

"Verus?"

"Yes, wife?" I sighed loudly as I poured a cup for her.

"I'm sorry. I'm extra grumpy when I'm hungry. I didn't mean to snap."

"It's fine," I replied brusquely, trying to ignore how something about her was softening the walls I was trying to keep up. Her apology almost made me feel bad for pushing her away, but I didn't want to give her the wrong idea. I would do my best to provide for her and her child—our child—but I had nothing else to offer.

Ari sat down at the table, and I brought her the tea. She looked up at me with her luminous eyes and smiled. "Thank you, husband."

It would be so much easier if we weren't stuck here together. She was the last thing I wanted or needed in my life. This week couldn't end quickly enough.

CHAPTER 6
MARITAL THINGS

ARIANWEN

One night turned into a week of awkwardly sharing a bed. By Argenti tradition, the first week of marriage was supposed to be spent holed up in our home, getting to know each other better. I was more than ready for the week to be over, especially when I discovered how restless of a sleeper Verus was. Almost every night, I'd find myself woken up with a foot lodged in my back or an arm flung across my face. I was starting to wonder if he was doing it on purpose to annoy me, but I held my tongue and just pushed him off whenever it happened.

In spite of everything, we settled into somewhat of a comfortable rhythm. Verus did most of the cooking, and I hated how good he was at it. I spent most of my time hidden away in my room, organizing the few belongings I had and re-reading the precious medical texts I'd smuggled home from Zephyria.

Being below the surface for so long was still not something I was familiar with. While I was loath to admit it, I'd gotten somewhat used to the bright, open skies of Zephyria. A wave of loneliness swept over me at the reminder of all I had left behind. I could vividly see Liisa's face as we'd laughed and worked together in the hospitium. Would she forgive me for leaving without saying goodbye? Not that I'd ever have a chance to find out. I would never return.

I desperately needed to get back to work. Staying home below the surface all day was driving me to madness. Perhaps I could convince Verus to go out for the day. Our week was almost over, and as long as we were together, I didn't think it would stir up too much trouble.

"Verus?" I called out as I made my way toward his room. I hadn't seen him since our shared breakfast earlier that morning. It wouldn't have surprised me if he were feeling stir-crazy too. I knocked on his door, calling out his name again.

"Yes?" he replied. I pushed the door open and found Verus lounging comfortably on his bed, reading a book, and looking utterly annoyed at the disturbance. "What do you want? I'm busy."

Clearing my throat, I replied, "Verus, I wanted to ask about maybe getting out of here for a change of scenery."

Verus rolled his eyes and sighed loudly as he set his book down. "What are you thinking?" He reached his arms behind his head in a stretch, his broad chest straining against the confines of his shirt.

Doing my best to ignore the sculpted muscles that drew my gaze down to where his shirt had ridden up, I forced my eyes to meet his, which was almost worse. His eyes were filled with irritation.

"I'm not meant to be cooped up in a house for an entire week! I need to get out and do something with all this pent-up energy."

"We're expected to be doing 'marital things,'" Verus said, his voice laced with sarcasm. He pinched the bridge of his nose as if warding off a headache.

"Well, can't we go do 'marital things' outside of the house?" I asked.

Verus huffed a laugh. "I'm fairly certain those things should not be done in public spaces unless you want to end up arrested."

"I meant *other* marital things." I rolled my eyes. "Don't married people go eat together or *something*?"

"I suppose we could go out to the market above and gather what we need to put a bed together for you."

I tapped my fingers on my chin and replied, "Gathering material for another bed hardly seems like something newly married people would be doing."

"Oh, you'd be surprised," Verus quipped.

My cheeks flushed red at the insinuation. Trying to push down my embarrassment, I shook my head. "Okay, fine, but keep in mind, we will need to pretend to somewhat like each other in case we run into any friends or relatives. If we want people to believe this child is yours, there can't be any question of the validity of our marriage."

Verus let out a long sigh. "You're probably right. The last thing we need is for the Iris to start poking around in our business."

"So it's agreed? I'm not beyond begging at this point. I really need to get out of this house."

"Agreed. I can't wait to have my bed to myself again."

After deciding to leave his seahorse and swim to the surface, we exited through the barrier that held the water at bay. There was pressure all around me before it gave way to the cold temperatures of the Iverian Sea. The water embraced me and instantly put me at ease. We should have gone swimming days ago, but I had been so focused on getting my room in order and avoiding Verus, it hadn't even crossed my mind as a possibility.

Verus grabbed my hand, and we sped toward the surface, the water guiding and pushing us along. When we'd arrived after our wedding, I'd been asleep, but now that I was fully awake, I paid more attention to our surroundings. There were many quaint, underwater homes near ours, and I saw younglings swimming about and playing together. It truly wasn't so different from my home above. If anything, it was far more peaceful, as the water muffled the noises of our neighbors.

As we neared the surface, Verus pulled me closer and placed an arm around my waist. Apparently, he'd taken my words about playing the part of a happily married husband to heart, but it still felt a little strange to be so close to him. The warmth of his hand seared through the thin fabric of my dress.

Once we broke through the surface, I put distance between us as I let the water roll down my body and rejoin the sea, siphoning the excess from my hair and clothes. I tried to ignore how Verus' eyes lingered on me, my clothes clinging to my curves. I couldn't truly fault him for looking, as my own gaze couldn't stop from wandering and admiring his muscular physique. He'd left his hair down, and he shook it in a playful manner, showering me with tiny droplets of water.

"Verus!" I couldn't help but laugh at his antics. He merely grinned before grabbing my hand and entwining our fingers as he led us into the city. The sudden change in personality was utterly jarring.

"Where would you like to go, *wife?*"

"I kind of thought you were leading the way, *husband*," I replied somewhat hesitantly.

"Well, then lead I shall."

We walked through the streets in awkward silence before heading into the market. Street vendors shouted about their current deals and wares, and Verus was continuously stopped by various acquaintances. Considering his usual demeanor around me, I was surprised at how well-liked he was. I found myself shying away from the attention, nodding as their congratulations were expressed, and flushing with embarrassment at the innuendos some of them threw our way about what we should be up to.

The summer sun was still beating down upon us as we walked through the stalls, and I felt sweat dripping down my back. While our main purpose was to pick up supplies for the bed, I was enjoying our casual stroll, admiring the unique artistry of random knickknacks and dyed fabrics on display.

Verus brought us to a food stall run by one of his friends, who he claimed made the most delicious fried crab cakes. The lump crab meat was sweet, briny, and seasoned just right—we devoured them.

Our exploration of the inner city markets continued at an unhurried pace, our satisfied bellies in combination with the day's heat enough to make me want to nap in the glassy water not too far from us. It would have been cool and refreshing as always, and I envied the Argenti who already took to those leisures. There wasn't a cloud in the sky, and the oppressive heat lingered stagnantly around us. We still needed to find the vendor who carried wood from the sawmill, so we continued on.

"Excuse me," I blurted as I bumped shoulders with a male. He responded with a rude glower before continuing past us in somewhat of a hurry. I almost doubted my eyes.

Did I just walk past Lucris, one of the highest ranking Argenti in Iveria? In this part of town? At this time of day?

Certainly he had servants in his employ who would have taken care of these types of errands. I shook my head, wondering at the strange occurrence.

Feeling overheated from the crowds in the market, I sought relief, fluttering the palm leaf fan Verus had so kindly bartered for after seeing me eye it a few stalls down.

A cool breeze picked up out of nowhere and caressed the back of my neck. The faint scent of pine and sage drifted over me, and I dropped my fan, twisting around to look.

It couldn't be. He wouldn't have.

My eyes roved around the crowd, searching for those icy blue eyes, but I didn't see him. Was I losing my mind?

"Is everything all right?" Verus asked before stooping down to pick up the fan I had dropped. "You look like a skittish seahorse." After handing me the fan, he tucked me under his arm, pressing a kiss to the top of my head. He sure knew how to put on an act.

My eyes continued to roam through the crowd. I truly must have been losing my mind. There was no way that he would have shown up here. I shook my head, covering my face with my hand. "I'm sorry, I don't know what is wrong with me. I thought maybe I scented someone . . ."

Verus chuckled. "There are so many scents in this market, I'd be surprised if you were able to pick out just one. Come. Let's go to one of my favorite places in the city."

"I'm sure you're right. I don't know what I was thinking. I guess I'm still out of sorts after everything that happened before we met."

When he didn't pry for more information, I tried to let it go, even as my eyes continued to scan the busy market. Despite the sun's harsh rays, a cool shiver made its way down my spine, and with it, a strange feeling of familiarity and memories I couldn't shake.

I'd made a choice to leave my past behind me, so I set my sights forward and followed Verus up the hill.

CHAPTER 7

Breaking the Bed

VERUS

It was surprisingly easy to pretend. When I wasn't being a complete arse, Arianwen was easy to talk to. Her smile lit up the world around her, and I realized she had not done much smiling in the past week. Not that we had spent a lot of time together. We had agreed not to speak of our pasts, but I had to admit, I was curious. Curious about the male who had so obviously hurt her, curious about why she would have sworn such a binding oath . . . but no. It was better to keep some distance between us.

For a moment, I'd almost let myself forget this wasn't real. What was I thinking?

We were halfway up the hill to the lookout I loved when I suddenly stopped. I couldn't share this with her. This was where I used to bring *her*.

"I changed my mind—let's head home," I said without preamble.

"What?" Arianwen looked at me incredulously. "We're nearly to the top of the hill! I'm sure the view is amazing this time of day."

"I said I'm ready to go." I turned and headed back down, not waiting to make sure she followed.

"Verus!" Arianwen called out in frustration.

Ignoring her, I continued walking. We couldn't afford to make a scene, and hopefully she'd realize that. The patter of her feet on the seastone street alerted me that she had finally decided to follow, but I was surprised when she grabbed my arm, jerking me to a stop.

"Verus! I was talking to you," she gritted out, trying to keep her voice low. "What in the stars is wrong with you? I thought we were having a nice time."

"I'm tired of pretending," I said under my breath, pulling my arm out of her grasp. "We should head back home."

"Fine," she replied. "I don't want to spend any more time with you either."

She started stalking off in the direction of the market, and I groaned. There were too many eyes around here. I hurried to catch up with her, grabbing her hand and matching her steps.

"What? Worried I'll leave you behind?" she snapped.

"Be pleasant, wife," I growled quietly. "Don't forget this was your idea."

"Already regretting it," she snarled, jabbing me slightly with her elbow.

"Verus! Is that you?" a familiar voice rang out from across the street.

Faex. Just what we need.

Slowing my steps, I put on a lazy smile and turned to greet my friends. "Tal. Koa. Nice to see you," I drawled.

"What are you and the wife doing out and about?" Koa teased.

"Yes, aren't you supposed to be enjoying yourselves at home?" Tal said suggestively, waggling his eyebrows.

"Oh, you know Verus," Arianwen said sweetly. "He really needed to take a break and get some fresh air . . ."

I almost choked on my breath. Where was she going with this?

My friends laughed loudly as she continued, "I think I wore the poor guy out."

"Darling," I crooned, "it's not nice to tell stories."

She turned to face me, placing her free hand on my chest, her eyes flashing in challenge. "I speak only the truth."

"We were just on our way to pick up materials for a new bed. Weren't we, *wife*?" I replied.

"Faex, Verus," Tal said, his shoulders shaking with laughter. "You'll have to share your secrets."

"Don't count on it," I replied.

"What a pity," Koa said before moving closer and holding his hand out to Arianwen. "I don't believe we had a chance to officially meet at your wedding. I'm Koa, Verus' best-looking friend."

I groaned in annoyance. Koa was way too flirtatious for his own good.

Arianwen released me and bypassed his extended hand, pulling him into a hug. "Any friend of Verus' is a friend of mine," she said sweetly. Koa folded her into his arms and winked at me over her shoulder.

My whole body tensed as I watched him embrace my wife. What in the depths was he trying to pull? And why was she allowing him to hug her like that? It took all my power to keep my face pleasant and not rip her out of his arms.

He finally let go, and she stepped back, but before she could go and try to hug Tal, I wrapped my arm around her shoulders and pulled her into my side. "We really need to be on our way. I think I've rested enough, if you know what I mean."

Arianwen snorted a quiet laugh, and I squeezed her closer.

"Try not to break any more beds, Verus," Tal quipped as he patted my shoulder and dragged Koa deeper into the market with him.

Watching my friends walk away, Arianwen sighed. "I guess we should go get those materials. I can't spend another night with your knees digging into my back."

"Well, I'm sick and tired of you stealing all the blankets," I huffed.

"Lead the way, husband," she said, pointing in the direction we needed to go.

CHAPTER 8
YOU'RE A TERRIBLE LIAR

ARIANWEN

To my utter surprise, Verus agreed to let me make dinner while he put the bed together for me. I'd thought the stars would fall out of the sky before he allowed me to cook for him.

Once I had finished preparing the meal, I headed back to my room to check on him and let him know it was ready.

I had to hold back a gasp when I opened the door and saw his shirtless body gleaming with sweat as he finished securing the wooden slats. The taut muscles of his back rippled and flexed with every movement as he worked. My jaw dropped open, and I couldn't help but admire his physique and the way his skilled hands made quick work of the task.

"Did you need something, wife?" Verus grunted as he continued working.

Get a hold of yourself, Ari! Stop drooling over your husband.

It felt somewhat ironic that I was chastising myself for feeling something for someone who I had every right to feel something for. It just didn't feel right to *me*. Hardly any time had passed since I'd left Wynn, and my heart was still in pieces. The last thing I needed was to give Verus the wrong impression and more reasons to be annoyed by me. Unfortunately, I could not deny the extreme physical attraction I felt to him. His deep, baritone voice and glistening body tried to wake parts of me I was desperate to keep slumbering.

My eyes were drawn to the elaborate whorls and swirls on his chest that looked like ocean waves crashing. I hadn't noticed the intricate runes woven into the markings until now, even though he often forgot to wear shirts.

When I didn't respond right away, he quipped, "My eyes are up here, wife."

A furious blush filled my cheeks. "I'm sorry . . . I got distracted by those markings. I don't recognize the language."

Verus' eyes glinted with surprising mirth. "Your jaw dropped so far, I thought I might have to pick it up off the floor. Don't mind me taking a little pleasure at the knowledge that you find me attractive."

"Who said anything about finding you attractive? Your markings are what fascinate me." I placed my hands on my hips, trying to regain a measure of composure. "Dinner is ready, and you stink of sweat. You should get cleaned up before you eat."

Verus stood and stepped closer to me before gently flicking my nose. "It's cute you think you can lie to me. You're a terrible liar, *wife*." He leaned closer and sniffed. "I can smell it all over you."

He straightened and winked, then turned on his heel toward the bathing room.

CHAPTER 9
A Healer's Calling

ARIANWEN

The expected time for our seclusion had passed, and I was more than happy to be able to visit my family. The previous week hadn't been all bad, but seeing them, especially my sister, sounded like a wonderful idea. Verus would be returning to work full time in the next few days, and I would need to find out how to complete my training as a healer without giving the Iris anything to worry about. As long as I was doing my duty by being married and growing a family, there was no reason I shouldn't be able to.

"Verus!" I called out as I left my room, tying off my braid while I walked toward the kitchen.

"In here," he replied.

I veered away from the kitchen and toward the front living area, following the sound of his voice. Verus was in his usual spot, lounging on the sofa, a cup of tea in hand while flipping through a book.

"Do you need something, Arianwen?" Verus asked, finally looking up at me.

"No, but I was going to let you know—now that our *seclusion* is officially over—I am heading out to visit my family."

He set his book down and tapped a finger on his chin. "Would you like me to come with you?"

Seriously? I might need to stop trying to figure this male out.

"Well . . . no, you don't have to," I said.

"I have to pick up some things before heading back to work, and we only have one seahorse," he grumbled. "Might as well just go and get it over with." He drained the remainder of his tea and stood up. "Is that acceptable to you, *wife?*"

I shrugged. "I suppose . . ."

"No supposing. Let's go," he said in a tone that left no room for argument. "I'll get Sterling ready."

After depositing his cup in the kitchen, he was out of the house before I could come up with an argument. I had kind of hoped to go on my own so I wouldn't have to put on a show of being happily married, but regardless, I was looking forward to seeing my family.

I followed Verus out to the small stable where he was bridling his beautiful seahorse. Sterling was midnight blue with streaks of shiny, orange pigment and was quite the handsome creature. Getting back onto a saddle with Verus had not been high on my list of things I'd been hoping to do today, but I took his proffered hand and climbed onto Sterling's back. Verus jumped on behind me and grabbed the reins. Within moments, we were off, speeding through the water faster than we could swim.

I closed my eyes, thinking about what I would say to my family, wondering how they would expect Verus and me to act. Was he going to come inside, or just drop me off and then take care of his business?

We broke through the surface of the water and guided Sterling to the dock near my family's home in one of the less densely packed areas of the capital. Verus jumped off, and I allowed him to help me dismount before he tied his seahorse to the post. While I wanted to dash to see my family, I decided waiting for him would be the polite thing to do. I also had to remind myself I no longer lived there. My home was with Verus, as I was a married female. I probably shouldn't barge into my family's house anymore.

It felt strange when I thought about being married. Perhaps it was because we were not really living as married people . . . but coming to my family's home with a husband, real or not, felt as if I were walking in someone else's skin. Especially after everything that had happened on my matri-ritus. I did not feel like the same girl who had left. I had been fundamentally changed by what I'd learned, and I wasn't sure if I would ever find myself again.

Verus walked up behind me and held out his arm for me to take. "We should keep up appearances," he murmured into my ear.

Out of habit, I looked around, and I spotted an Iris patrol meandering. Their metallic breastplates and boots made the luminous marbling in their skin gleam even brighter—walking symbols of what we served. We'd been led to believe they were our shining saviors sent by the stars, but I knew the truth.

I'd never been sure how much they actually paid attention to us and how they kept tabs on what we were doing. Weren't there too many of us? How could they possibly keep track?

Verus and I casually started walking down the dock toward the row of houses where my family lived when a sudden commotion drew our attention.

A female with tear-stricken cheeks and ragged clothing appeared to be begging as she knelt on the ground before an Iris guard. I couldn't hear the words she was saying, but her cries reached me, and I flinched as the guard knocked her across the head with the butt of his sword. I stood frozen as she fell backward onto the ground with a dull thud. Her body lay limp, even as the Iris guard kicked her in the stomach repeatedly. He sneered down at her and walked away, as if her life meant nothing.

"Stars, we need to do something!" I said turning to look at Verus, but he was already running across the street toward where the Iris guard had gone. I hurried over to the female and knelt next to her, feeling for a pulse. She'd hit her head on the seastone pavement, but she was still breathing and her pulse was steady, giving me the slightest modicum of relief.

Verus returned and stood watch, concern etching his features. "What do we do, Arianwen? Should we take her somewhere? Get help?"

"We can't move her just yet," I said. "I need to try to stabilize her first."

I checked her pupils, then glided my fingers over her head, probing with my magic while also focusing on feeding it into her to repair the damage. My eyes flicked to her abdomen where she'd been kicked, and I could sense the broken ribs and internal bleeding. It was too much for me to fix on my own.

"She has injuries that I don't know how to treat," I muttered, then I pointed across the street. "The hospitium is that way. Get help! Hurry!"

I focused on her head injury—so long as I could preserve her most vital organ, she stood a chance at surviving. The female's eyes fluttered, and I gasped in surprise as she returned to consciousness and groaned. Flooded with emotion, I held back tears at seeing her revival. It felt like ages since I'd saved a life, and only seconds ago, I'd begun doubting my ability. The female began moaning in pain, guarding her midsection, then screamed with her sudden movement.

"Shhh . . . it's all right." I sent another wave of healing power into her, focusing on her ribs this time. "I'm here to help," I said calmly. "Please try not to move."

She shuddered in response and grasped on to my skirt with a free hand, her knuckles going white with the pain she was holding back. I looked up in the direction Verus had run, hoping he'd found the hospitium, praying he'd be back soon.

The female was hyperventilating as she held back sobs, and her eyes became unfocused as though she might pass out again.

"What's your name?" I asked, trying to keep her with me.

"Marwen," she gritted through rapid breaths. "I was just trying to feed my family . . . I volunteered to go to Prisma, but they wouldn't take me . . . said I was too weak."

I cursed under my breath. I'd seen more than enough to know that the Iris truly weren't the great benefactors they wanted us to believe they were. Judging by Marwen's emaciated appearance and worn out clothes, she wasn't lying. So many Argenti families were starving and living in overcrowded homes due to the Iris' unreasonable marriage laws. The stars had blessed most of our people with large families, but space was limited. The city's population was overflowing with Argenti who did not have the means to provide for their families.

"You did nothing wrong," I said to her. "Just hang in there. We're going to get you help."

Waiting for Verus to return, though it may have only been minutes, felt like hours. I began fearing he'd gotten lost.

"Move away from her," an oily sounding voice commanded from behind me.

CHAPTER 10
FAKE IT 'TIL YOU MAKE IT

ARIANWEN

I froze, not wanting to leave Marwen alone but also scared not to listen to who I assumed was the Iris guard.

I turned my head to look briefly, and anger at him for kicking a female who had already been down simmered within me. The needless suffering he and other Iris inflicted upon countless Argenti for the pettiest of crimes—crimes they shouldn't have to commit in the first place—was disgusting. I looked back to the female, whose eyes widened in fear upon seeing him. I would not leave her side.

"You got a problem with your hearing or something? I said move away," he snarled, approaching us in a rage.

I did the only thing I could do and curled my body over her protectively. I was braced for his attack when commotion up the street distracted the guard, the armored click of his footsteps coming to a halt. I stole a glance up to see Verus running down the street pulling a wagon, a male and female healer running after him.

"Don't come any closer," the guard said.

Verus slowed his pace as he neared, but he did not stop. The guard's shoulders stiffened as he realized he was losing control of the situation.

Verus dropped the wagon pull and rushed past me, putting himself between the guard and us. I was sure he made an intimidating picture with his height rivaling that of the Iris guard. The bulk of his muscles would hopefully give him an advantage as well.

"She needs help," he said calmly. "My wife is a healer and is merely doing her job."

I held Marwen's hand and nodded to her reassuringly, then slowly turned and looked up at the Iris guard again, his sneer turning his beautiful face into something dark and malevolent.

"She deserved what she got," he spat. "I came back to drag her to the brig."

"Surely she is no risk to you," Verus replied, his deep voice calm and measured with a note of warning. He took another step toward the guard, creating more space between us. I tried not to flinch, worrying that standing up to the Iris would only get Verus punished instead, but the guard appeared to become more and more uncomfortable as Verus encroached upon him. "She is barely conscious. Please, let us get her the help she needs. Surely she has paid enough retribution for any crime committed."

The Iris guard looked down at her and back at Verus, and I was surprised when he suddenly took a step back. He growled, "She's not worth the paperwork. When I return, she better be gone, or you all will be headed to the brig." He turned on his heel and went the opposite direction.

I couldn't help but heave a giant sigh of relief. "I don't know whether I should throttle you or hug you for what you just did," I said quietly under my breath.

Verus let out a strangled laugh. "Someone needs to stand up to those pricks. Beating a helpless female does not command respect. Are you all right? He didn't harm you?" His eyes scanned over me.

I shook my head before closing my eyes for a brief moment, grateful the stars had been on our side this once.

As soon as the guard was out of sight, the healers rushed over to help.

"I don't know how much time that guard will give us before he returns," I said. "Help me get her into the wagon."

Verus nodded and went to fetch the wagon.

The senior healer shook her head as she approached, looking appalled at what had been done to the poor female.

"You didn't move her, did you?" she asked, looking at me.

"No. She has some cracked ribs and abdominal trauma, but I'm most concerned about her head injury. She hit it on the seastone and lost consciousness for a time, but I was able to manage some of the bleeding and reduce the swelling. She may have more extensive injuries which I don't know how to detect or treat."

The healer knelt down next to her, probing with her own magic, and asked Marwen, "Can you move your toes, dear?"

She groaned and rasped a soft "yes."

Verus eased the wagon over to us, and the apprentice grabbed a rolled-up fabric stretcher which he set down beside the patient.

"Can you help us take her back to the hospitium? I'm afraid we won't make it in time without your help."

"Of course," Verus replied.

The four of us transferred the patient onto the stretcher and lifted it up into the wagon. I stood, summoning some water to wash the blood off my hands as the apprentice took over care of Marwen.

"Are you a healer?" the older female asked me. "I haven't seen you in the hospitium."

I shook my head. "I haven't completed my training, but I am hoping to continue learning if there are any openings for me."

"You are calm under pressure. I like that," the healer replied as she climbed up into the wagon with Marwen. "Come to the hospitium tomorrow and ask for me, Quilla. I will make sure there is room for you."

I blinked in surprise, and a warm smile of gratitude graced my face. "Thank you, Quilla. I will."

She nodded and turned to her apprentice. "Marcus, please help with the wagon."

"I'll meet you at your family's home," Verus said as he picked up the other side of the wagon pull and started guiding it toward the hospitium.

I watched them go for a moment, grateful that the stars had seen us here at the right moment to save Marwen and that the three of us were not being imprisoned, or worse.

As I walked slowly toward my family's home, I wished—as I often did—that I could do more. Wynn had told me that those who are desperate find each other. Would I be able to discover the rebels here in Iveria and find a way to help? Was Verus a rebel? The way he had stood up to the Iris had surprised me—that he'd been willing to risk so much for a stranger.

Before I could knock, the door flew open, and my sister threw her arms around me.

"Ari! What are you doing here? It's so good to see you," she said as she practically squeezed the air out of my lungs and ushered me into the house. "How is married life treating you? You look well enough."

"Lani, how do you expect me to answer when you keep peppering me with questions?" I teased.

She laughed, and my heart warmed, grateful to be reunited with my sister, even if only for a few hours. We walked into the kitchen where my mother was preparing tea.

"Hello, Mother," I said and gave her a quick kiss on the cheek. "Are the boys home?"

"Ari, what a pleasant surprise," she replied. "Your father is working, of course, but your brothers should be back from their chores any moment now. Are you well? You look extra pale. You're not eating enough."

"I'm fine, Mother," I said, biting my tongue to keep myself from talking back.

"Take a seat!" she commanded. "I've made tea and biscuits."

"Sounds wonderful, thank you."

Lani dragged me over to the round kitchen table, and we sat next to each other. The biscuits smelled fresh and divine. I picked one up and broke off a piece, moaning with happiness at the flaky, buttery taste. "Mother, these are incredible. You must give me your recipe."

She chuckled, her face glowing at the praise as she filled three cups with tea and came over to join us.

"Okay, Ari. *You* must finally answer my questions," Leilani said, giving me her no-nonsense look.

"Of course, *sister*," I replied after stuffing one more bite of biscuit into my mouth. "To answer your first question, I am here because I missed you all, of course."

My mother rolled her eyes and clucked her tongue at me. "You're married now, darling."

"I know, I just . . . I've missed you all, especially after being gone for so long. Verus' home just doesn't feel quite like my home yet. And it is so different being below all the time. But I think I can learn to love it, even if we aren't there for much longer. My source is never low, being surrounded by our element at all times."

Lani squeezed my hand. "I can't even begin to imagine . . . but your husband . . ." Her eyes gleamed with curiosity and excitement. "Mother and Father sure made a wonderful match for you. I can only hope that there is such a handsome male available for me next year. Does Verus have any attractive friends?"

I felt myself blushing. I could not deny how handsome Verus actually was. "No, I am not introducing you to them, but yes, he is quite pleasant to look at."

"And he's taking good care of you?" Lani waggled her eyebrows suggestively.

"Lani!" I exclaimed, knocking her hand away. "I'm not discussing that with you." I darted my eyes toward our mother, appalled that she would bring that up in front of her, taking a large sip of my tea.

My mother rolled her eyes at me again. "As if I don't know what married people do." She tsked. "It's a perfectly reasonable question. I hope he was gentle with you. I'd assume by the size—"

"Stop, please, Mother!" I gasped as tea almost came out my nose.

Lani doubled over, howling in amusement, and I couldn't help but let out a strangled laugh. If someone had told me I'd be sitting at a table with my mother and sister, joking about my husband's ability to *care* for me, I would have sworn they were losing their minds.

A knock at the door had me straightening in my seat. "That's probably Verus," I explained as my mother got up quickly and went to answer it.

"Why didn't you tell us he was coming?" Lani asked with excitement.

I rolled my eyes. "Need I remind you, dear sister, that you've barely even let me speak since I came in the door. Not to mention all your teasing about—"

My mother cleared her throat loudly as she entered the room, giving me a stern look. I guessed the time for joking about Verus' bedroom skills had passed.

"Please, take a seat," she said as she bustled off to prepare another cup of tea.

"Did everything go all right at the hospitium?" I asked.

"Yes, we had no trouble," Verus replied as he came over and surprised me by pressing a kiss to the top of my head before dropping into the seat on the other side of me. His large frame took up so much space, and the feeling of his thigh pressing into mine underneath the table caused a brief shiver of awareness to come over me. He slung his arm around the back of my chair, and his hand gently squeezed my shoulder.

My sister noted everything with wide eyes, from how close to me he was sitting to the casual way he was showing affection.

This is just him selling the idea that we are happily matched, I reminded myself. Hopefully my mother and sister would spread the word that things were good between us.

"Why were you at the hospitium?" Leilani asked.

"The Iris beat up a female just outside when we arrived," Verus explained. "I ran to get help while Arianwen stabilized her. The healer said if Arianwen hadn't acted so quickly, the female might have suffered permanent injuries." He gently tugged at my braid, sending more shivers through me as he looked at me and smiled.

I couldn't help but blush at the praise. "I only did what anyone else would have done in my shoes."

"I can't believe you ran to help her," Lani gasped. "What if the Iris had seen you and come after you too?"

My mother gave me a worrying glance, as if she were remembering the last time I had caught the attention of the Iris.

I looked over at Verus, a question in my eyes. Should we tell them the whole story? He gently shook his head, and I straightened my posture, willing strength into my voice. "I would have never forgiven myself if I had stood by and done nothing."

"Arianwen was incredible out there. She knew exactly what to do, and she saved a life."

I looked down at my hands, the unexpected praise sending heat to my cheeks once again, making me wonder for a moment if he had meant it. He'd seemed sincere. If he hadn't been, his acting skills were impressive.

"Well, I, for one, am glad it all worked out," my mother finally chimed in as she brought Verus his tea. "I hear from Lev that you're nearly done with your apprenticeship. That's faster than most, and he says you show great potential. I trust you'll be moving closer very soon."

He accepted her compliments graciously, and we proceeded to make small talk around the table. Once my brothers showed up, they showered Verus with all manner of questions about his work with my father. His answers were good-natured and thoughtful, which brought another rush of warmth into my heart. Our marriage might not be real, and he didn't actually appear to like me, but he seemed like a good person deep down. He set my family at ease with how caring he was in their presence.

If only he could show me some of that at home.

For the rest of the afternoon his small affections continued, which brought confusing feelings to the surface. I knew it was all for show, but my body didn't seem to accept that. I'd have been lying if I didn't admit that it was nice to feel like a treasured wife, even for just a few hours. Perhaps I shouldn't have agreed to this.

Wynn's rejection had stung so bitterly. His choosing Katye had made me feel as if I would never be deserving of someone's sole affection. Even though I knew this wasn't real, Verus was so very good at pretending that it almost felt like it was.

CHAPTER 11
RENEWED PURPOSE

ARIANWEN

The next day, I made my way to Iveria's central hospitium to meet with Quilla. Verus had returned to work, and I was itching to get back to my own training. Being able to study at the hospitium would be a huge honor and would allow me to learn much more than at my first apprenticeship. After disappearing for months, the healer I'd worked with had given my position to someone else.

The streets of Iveria were bustling with life as children rushed off to their schools and market vendors dragged their carts full of wares behind them. I tried to remind myself to breathe as anxiety crept in, the desire to make a good impression overwhelming. As I walked into the doors of the hospitium, I was reminded again how much more clinical the environment was compared to the hospitium in Zephyria. I had only been here a few times while assisting my old mentor, because only the most serious cases came to the hospitium. Most Argenti were attended by healers at their homes for less severe illnesses and injuries.

The scent of medicinal herbs made my sensitive nose twitch as I searched for someone to direct me to Quilla. I also wanted to check on Marwen and see how she was recovering. She had mentioned trying to feed her family, and I couldn't help but wonder if there was anyone taking care of them, or if they knew what had happened.

I stood there for a moment, taking in the sight of healers and aids hustling throughout the great hall, imagining myself in their shoes.

"You appear lost. Can I help you?" a young male asked, his voice lacking enthusiasm. He appeared to be an apprentice on scut work, if his uniform and cloudy disposition were any indication. After telling him who I was there to see, he gave me a jealous-looking once-over, then pointed me in the right direction.

Knocking softly on her door, I heard a muffled reply tell me to enter.

"Good morning," I said as I walked into Quilla's small office. "I'm Arianwen S—Kalani," I said, remembering my last name had changed with my marriage to Verus. "We met yesterday near the coral port."

"Oh, yes, of course," she said with a smile as she waved me in. "You saved a life yesterday, and it would be foolish of me to let a talented healer like you slip through my fingers."

I smiled, trying to gracefully accept the compliment. "Thank you, ma'am."

"Please call me Quilla," she insisted. "Marwen was able to return home this morning thanks to your quick action, in case you were wondering."

"That's wonderful news," I said. "I had hoped to visit her, but I am glad she was able to return home. She seemed very concerned for her family, and I only wish I could have done more."

Quilla's posture stiffened. "I hope we didn't patch her up just to see her end up in an Iris brig after all. Sadly, more and more Argenti are getting desperate and making foolish choices because they are unable to provide for their families."

I nodded, trying to push back the feeling of hopelessness at the sobering reality. Just because we had managed to heal her didn't mean she would suddenly have the ability to care for her family. If I were still with my former mentor, I would have been out in the community and perhaps had the opportunity to help more people like her. Working in the hospitium might actually limit my ability to help . . . yet I wasn't sure I could turn down the chance to learn here. The skills I developed in this apprenticeship could make a difference later. Was there a way I could do both?

I also had my child to think about. Time had a way of speeding past, and I'd most likely need to step back from my work to take care of him or her. As it so often happened, I was stuck between wanting to be able to do everything, and I was uncertain if it would even be possible.

"So, my dear," Quilla continued, "remind me again what your experience has been thus far?"

"I was working as an apprentice before I was wed, but my place was given to someone else while I was on my matri-ritus." I paused, thinking about all the experience I could never share. *Stars-damned oath*. "I have a strong desire to be out in the community using my gifts, but I also want to learn as much as I can. Would both of those things be possible here?"

"You are newly wed, I assume?" she asked.

"Yes, only a few weeks now," I replied, wondering what that had to do with anything.

She tapped her nails on her desk as she considered. "It can be done, but it won't be easy in your condition." She glanced at my stomach with a knowing look.

My eyes widened in surprise. "Is it that obvious?"

Quilla let out a soft laugh. "Don't look so worried, my dear. My years of experience have honed my senses more than the average healer."

Relief washed over me with the knowledge that I wouldn't have to try to defend or explain myself to her. I'd come to this meeting with fears that she might not want to waste her time teaching me once she learned of my condition.

"Keep in mind," she continued, "it will require long hours, a lot of time on your feet, and some sacrifices at home. So long as you're aware of what you are getting yourself into, I'd hate to turn you away. You are a natural healer, it's clear, I just want to make sure you are fully aware of the commitment you are agreeing to."

I squeezed my hands in my lap, attempting to nod where appropriate. Healing meant everything to me—I didn't know who I was if not a healer. I'd have hidden my pregnancy as long as possible if it had come to that. Knowing I wouldn't have to was the confirmation I needed that I was in the right place.

"I have an experienced healer you can work with here," Quilla said. "She does a lot of house calls for some of the wealthier Argenti, which will be safer for both you and your child." Picking up on the drop in my expression, she continued, "I know it's not what you were asking for. I know your type—you want to do everything, help everyone, but I trust the experience will be invaluable to you. If you work hard, you could be sent out on your own within the year. I would still like you to be here in the hospitium once or twice a week so you can gain experience with some of the more challenging cases. How does that sound?"

I mulled it over briefly, regretting my inability to hide my disdain of the *wealthier* Argenti, as Quilla had put it. While most Argenti worked incredibly hard to try to make ends meet, there were a few families who had roots leading back to Court of Water royalty and had been allowed to maintain some of their wealth in exchange for working closely with the Iris and helping carry out their agenda. Despite my hesitation, healing *was* my purpose, and I would feel lost without it. If I wanted to learn from the best, this was the place to do so. The sooner I could complete my training, the sooner I could help those whom I wanted to help.

"Sounds good to me," I replied, my voice as firm as my resolve.

"Wonderful," she said. "You can start today. Follow me, and I'll introduce you to Dalia."

Trudging through the streets later that evening, the weight of the day pressing down on me, I made my way toward where our seahorse was stabled. My mind drifted to my trainer, Dalia, who had been tough but fair. I knew I was going to be challenged in many ways with my new apprenticeship. She was no Pluvia or Liisa, but I had a feeling we would work well together. I was looking forward to getting back to work, even though it had worn me out. Anything to distract my mind and help me forget.

The exhaustion from being on my feet all day hit me as I dove into the water's welcoming embrace toward the stable below. I warily approached our grumpy seahorse to saddle him for the ride home, glad to see he hadn't finished all the food I'd left him. Even with my animal affinity, Sterling was extremely loyal to Verus, and I could have sworn he rolled his eyes at me whenever I approached him.

Notwithstanding his attitude, I was grateful Verus had insisted on me taking him. I'd tried to argue against it, but he had merely flicked his eyes to my stomach as if that were reason enough, and there was no swaying him. He was such a papa goose—so grumpy yet protective of his family, despite how everything between us was still uncertain and new.

I shivered a little after pushing through the barrier into our home and quickly siphoned the water out of my clothes and hair before sending it back out into the sea. Something smelled delicious, and my rumbling stomach reminded me that I had barely eaten since breakfast.

"I'm home!" I said brightly, as I stepped into the kitchen.

Verus merely grunted, but I shook it off as I made my way toward my bedroom to change into something more comfortable. I was grateful to have ended up with a male who enjoyed spending time cooking, even if he was an arse about it half the time. Maybe he could show me some things, as I had not spent nearly as much time learning from my mother as I should have. I quickly swapped out my work shift for my favorite sweater and walked back toward the kitchen.

"Smells incredible," I said, joining Verus at the hearth where he was stirring something.

"Come stir this for me," he said before handing me the spoon. A subtle spark shot through me as our hands brushed, causing me to look up to see if he had noticed. When he didn't react, I shook it off.

"Thank you for making dinner," I said while stirring the contents of the pot.

He sighed loudly. "I would have made it regardless. I need to eat too," he replied while carefully removing a thick, crusted bread from a clay pot over the hearth.

"I know . . . but I can't help but feel bad that you're always cooking. I should make food for you too sometimes."

He walked up behind me and peeked into the pot. "That should be good."

"Can I try it?" I asked, scooping some into the spoon, not waiting for an answer and bringing it to my mouth.

"Ari—"

"Faex! That's hot," I blurted out as the stew burned my tongue.

Verus sighed. "I was trying to warn you."

I looked up at him sheepishly, handing back the spoon. "What I managed to taste was good."

He rolled his eyes, and I thought I saw the hint of a smile trying to emerge before he turned around to grab some bowls.

Despite the fact that we could barely stand each other most of the time, Verus did seem to care about my well-being. My heart was still a mess after everything that had happened, but I couldn't deny that there was *something* between us. Maybe it was just attraction, but even with his often cranky exterior, I knew there was a kind male underneath. When I thought about how he had stood up to the Iris the day before, it stirred up feelings of respect. I wanted to know him better, in spite of how much he usually tried to push me away.

Would it be so bad to try to care for him that way?

No. That's ridiculous. We'd drive each other insane.

I sighed to myself as I filled two glasses with water and brought them to the table. Maybe someday we'd manage to get along for more than a few minutes.

As we sat down, Verus surprisingly asked me about my day and listened with a markedly piqued interest when I told him about my experiences.

"Do you remember that male I bumped into in the market last week?"

Verus shook his head before raising a spoonful of stew to his mouth.

"Well, I'm fairly certain his name is Lucris. Dalia took me to attend to his wife, Heather, who is expecting a child."

"Why do you bring it up?" Verus asked with a raised brow.

"I don't know . . . I just got a weird feeling about him when we saw him in the market."

Verus shrugged, and I shook it off.

"Anyway, I hope I don't have to spend much more time in the wealthier areas. I'd really love to be out in the community where my gifts are most needed, and I think the plan Quilla came up with is the quickest way to make that happen. When I think of all the other Marwens out there who could use my help, I can't ignore this feeling of urgency to finish my training so I can be out there assisting them. Marwen wasn't even the worst of them. If you'd seen half of what I've seen . . . The Iris can be so brutal." I shuddered.

Verus nodded in agreement. "What you want to do is very commendable, but don't be so hard on yourself. You are only one person—you can't be expected to save everyone."

His words reminded me of losing my first patient and how much that had hurt. How I'd had to learn that sometimes, in spite of all my best efforts, there would be some who were beyond saving. And I was still learning to accept that, even though everything inside me rebelled against it.

"Let me know how I can help," Verus said, pulling me from my dark thoughts.

The authenticity in his eyes and sincere willingness to help touched me, giving me an idea. Verus was right. I couldn't save everyone, but I would try to help as many as I could.

"Do you think I could maybe bring some of this stew and bread to Marwen and her family? One of the healers at the hospitium told me where she lives so I could check on her."

"I think that's a wonderful idea," Verus replied almost immediately. "I'm afraid that Iris guard has it out for her and will be watching for another opportunity to prove his point. The last thing she needs to be doing is risking his notice while scavenging for food."

I felt my cheeks heat in anger. "It's not right. If they truly were our great benefactors sent by the stars . . ." My hand burned slightly at even the thought of revealing information I had learned in Zephyria, and I growled in frustration. "They just . . . They should do more for us."

Verus raised his eyebrows, looking perplexed at my reaction. "We don't have a ton leftover, but I will pack up whatever I can, and you can bring it by tomorrow. I'm sure it will be appreciated."

I smiled at him, reaching over to squeeze his hand. "Thank you, Verus. Thank you for understanding."

He stiffened, looking down at my hand before pulling his away. "It's nothing."

CHAPTER 12

STICKY FINGERS

ARIANWEN

Needing a sense of normalcy, I snuck out of our home early one morning, deciding to visit the market for breakfast and perhaps spend the rest of my day in the only library the Argenti had access to. For a moment, I allowed myself to think about Zephyria's magnificent library and how I could have spent hours immersed in it, but it only caused me to remember what I'd lost.

I had just completed my first full week of work with Dalia, and spending my day off around my grumpy husband sounded less than ideal. It's not like he would miss me. It's hard to miss someone you can barely stand the sight of, and considering how often he hid in his room when we were both home, the message was loud and clear.

Should I have asked Verus if I can take Sterling out today? I thought to myself as I readied his harness. *Perhaps. But it's not like he has anywhere to be. Should I have left a note saying where I was going? Maybe. But after the way he ignored me last night, I'm not feeling generous enough to share my whereabouts.*

The sun was barely showing its face when I emerged from the water in the coral port near my family's home. While I wasn't planning on stopping by to see them, this was the closest port to my favorite market.

The streets were waking as the weekend vendors started setting up their wares. The smell of cinnamon and sugar wafted by, and my mouth watered. A sticky bun sounded perfect, so I quickly made my way to the small pastry shop whose doors were open to allow the delicious aroma to entice anyone nearby.

"Good morning, Gerard!" I said cheerfully as I entered the shop.

"Well, if it isn't Arianwen! Look who's brightening up the store as always," the kindly, older fae said, busy at work and covered in flour.

"It feels like it's been forever since I've had one of your delicacies," I said with a smile.

"Didn't you get married recently?" he asked, his gaze drifting past my shoulder. "Is your husband with you?"

I wrinkled my nose in irritation before remembering that gossip had a way of making its rounds, and I fixed my face into a more pleasant visage. "Not today, Gerard. He works very hard, so he's taking the day to rest at home."

"Oh, what a shame. I would've liked to meet him," he replied.

It took everything in my power not to roll my eyes. While my husband seemed to have some redeeming qualities, he was such an arse half the time.

"I'll be sure to bring him by soon," I lied through my teeth. Definitely not if I had anything to say about it.

"Well then, what can I get you?"

"Two sticky buns to go, please," I said, bouncing on my heels.

"Of course, of course. I'll make sure to wrap them up so they'll make it home safely. I heard you moved below, isn't that right?"

I had every plan to demolish at least one bun before I left the market, but he didn't need to know that.

"Yes, we live closer to the city center," I replied.

"Oh, you're quite far from home then," he said, a hint of derision in his tone. "I'm surprised your parents didn't make a better match for you."

Feeling oddly defensive, I quipped, "Verus is a wonderful male, and he's rising in the ranks at the shipyard with my father."

Gerard huffed haughtily. "Well, that explains it, I suppose. I thought for sure you'd marry someone like my boy, Thomas."

As friendly as Gerard normally was, there was no way in the depths I would have agreed to marry his son. We had gone to school together, and that boy had tormented me to no end. Gerard must have been losing his grasp on his faculties if he thought the two of us would have made a good match.

"I hope you find a lovely wife for Thomas before the end of the year," I said, starting to question myself for returning to my old stomping grounds.

The familiar sound of jingling bracelets had me turning my head and quickly regretting it. Of all the fae to walk through the door, it had to be my Aunt Rakhilit. She loved to pile on as much jewelry as possible to show off her station, and her bangles always announced her arrival.

"Ari, darling, what are you doing on this side of town?" she asked as she came over to embrace me, blowing small air kisses at my cheeks.

"Just picking up breakfast," I replied, still holding on to my bitterness at her for how she'd been gossiping about me at my own wedding.

Her eyes went to the sticky buns Gerard was wrapping up. "You know, sweetheart, just because you're married doesn't mean you shouldn't be careful about what you're eating. It's your responsibility to keep your husband interested."

My eyes widened in shock at the brazenness and utter wrongness of what she was saying. At a loss for words, I stood staring at her, my mouth hanging open as I tried to come up with the right response.

"Personally, I think she's perfect and has no trouble keeping my attention," Verus said, his voice dripping with pride.

What in the stars is he doing here? Did he follow me?

I couldn't decide if I was happy for the backup or mad that he was intruding on my day to myself.

"I thought you said your husband was resting at home," Gerard blurted out.

"I decided to surprise my darling wife." Verus winked at me as he stepped closer, pulling me into his side.

"How lovely," Aunt Rakhilit said unapologetically. "How is married life treating you?"

Pasting a smile on my face, I wrapped my arm around Verus, squeezing a little too hard. "It's perfect, Aunt." I reached over to the counter to grab the pastries, then disentangled myself from Verus. "I'll meet you outside," I said to him before turning back to the counter. "My husband will pay you, Gerard. It was nice to see you. Goodbye, Aunt." I hurried out of the shop, needing to get away from the suffocating judgment.

Hoping to possibly avoid Verus, I darted through the busy market and dipped down a side street. The thrill and excitement of my escape surged through me, and I let out a hysterical laugh at the ridiculousness of it. I unwrapped one of the sticky buns and inhaled the sweet, buttery aroma that had my mouth watering again. My aunt's comments had gotten under my skin, but I wasn't going to allow her to get into my head. Perhaps hiding from Verus was childish, but I really didn't want to face him.

I tore off a piece of the bun and moaned at the explosion of buttery goodness that overwhelmed my senses. As much as Gerard had annoyed me, he really made the best pastries.

"You stole my seahorse, wife," an unwelcome voice gritted out.

I groaned, closing my eyes for a moment. "Aren't we married, husband? Isn't he *our* seahorse?" I flashed my eyes toward him in challenge.

Verus reached over and grabbed the bag with the other sticky bun in it. When I glared at him, he shrugged. "What? I bought it, didn't I?"

"I was saving that one for later," I said with a pout, attempting to snatch the bag back from him, which he too easily lifted out of my reach. "What in the deep are you even doing here? Did you follow me?"

"Imagine my surprise waking up to a missing wife and seahorse," he replied, opening the pastry bag to look inside. "I thought you might be visiting your family, so I came here and found you in the market," he explained as if it were simple.

"Why do you even care?" I blurted out. "No one is around—you don't have to pretend to want to spend time with me."

Verus sighed loudly as he ran one hand through his hair. "I was planning on going out to the isles to visit some friends, but as I said, missing seahorse . . ."

"Oh." I bit my lip. "I'm sorry for not checking if you had any plans."

Verus' eyes darted toward my mouth before flashing up to my eyes. "It's fine, but it would be nice if you let me know in the future before disappearing with our only seahorse."

"That's fair."

Verus took a large bite of the extra sticky bun, and I frowned.

"What? I had to rush after you—I didn't have time for breakfast."

CHAPTER 13

Verus Gets Deep

VERUS

"Verus! I'm home!" a cheerful voice called out from the mud-room.

I sighed, wanting to run and hide in my room for the rest of the evening, or maybe I could make an excuse and go hang out with Tal. It had been a few months of living with this female, and despite the sadness and despair that had been written all over her face when we'd first met, she was somehow rediscovering her joy. Even with all of my attempts to avoid her, she still smiled and tried to make me smile too. It was getting harder and harder to push her away.

I found myself enjoying her presence more than hating it, questioning whether it was still a betrayal. She was worming her way into the shredded remains of my heart, and I was finding it difficult to keep her out.

"How was your day?" she chirped as she put away seaberries and greens she must have foraged on her way home.

"The same as usual," I said as I focused on the herbs I was mincing to throw into the evening's stew.

She turned to me, rolling her eyes in the adorable way she often did when I refused to let her in. "You're saying that absolutely nothing of note happened today?"

"Yep," I replied, trying to focus on my task, but her scent—the lavender that seemed to cling to her no matter what—infiltrated my nose.

"Are things still going well with your apprenticeship?"

While I rationally knew she was just trying to be friendly, another part of me wondered if she was getting tired of living below and wanted to return to her life above. I had been working my arse off to save for a better home, but it would take more time.

She sighed loudly when I didn't reply. "I suppose I'll change into something more comfortable for dinner. Thank you, as always, for making it."

I grunted a response. I enjoyed cooking—it gave me something to focus on, something to do with my hands, especially when they'd rather be wrapped up in her hair and pulling her close.

Faex. I shook my head, trying to dismiss the intrusive thoughts. It had been far too long since I'd been with someone.

We were married, and I had no idea how she'd respond if I tried to come on to her. It wasn't that I feared she'd reject the idea. I'd sensed her arousal before and the noticeable way she blushed, but I also didn't want to give her the wrong impression. I would never be able to give her the deep connection she so clearly deserved—I just wanted release. Stars knew I needed it.

It didn't help that her scent drove me wild with desire. I wanted to taste her, take my time exploring every dip and curve of her hips, and feel the swell of her breasts pressed up against me. Her fiery attitude only made me more attracted to her, and I couldn't help imagining how it would translate to other activities.

Attraction would never be a problem between us. The number of nights I spent with my hand gripped around myself, wishing it was hers, faex. What would she think of me?

I threw the herbs into the pot, stirring them up, allowing the smell to invade my senses and remove her scent from my nose. More spice, that's what it needed. Perhaps it might dissuade her sensual moans that threatened to undo me with every meal. Those moans of delight, the smallest trinkets of reward I'd secretly begun to crave, in spite of myself.

I heard her soft footsteps behind me, and once again, her torturous scent flooded my senses.

I swear to the stars, if she is wearing one of her flimsy nightgowns again, I will throw her on the table and have my way with her right here and now.

I turned to grab a pair of bowls and let my eyes wander to where she stood, leaning against the doorframe. Was it relief or disappointment I was feeling that she only wore loose-fitting pants and a slouchy sweater?

"Would you like me to set the table?" she asked with a demure smile.

"Just go ahead and sit down," I replied. "I'll serve it up and bring it over."

"Sounds good. Thank you," she said as she sank into one of the chairs. "I had the longest day today. I didn't even have a moment to eat any of the food I packed."

"That's unacceptable." I scoffed. "You need to take better care of yourself and our child."

I could almost feel her rolling her eyes behind me. "I'll try harder tomorrow."

"See that you do," I said as I ladled the stew and grabbed our spoons. Steam wafted from the bowls as I set them carefully on the table. "Better blow on it first," I warned before turning to grab two glasses of water.

"Oh my stars, Verus," Arianwen groaned in delight. "You completely outdid yourself this time."

Her groans went straight to my cock, so I spun back around to grab a loaf of bread and quickly slid into my chair before she could see just how much she was affecting me.

"Just what I wanted," she exclaimed with delight as she grabbed the bread, ripping off a large chunk before dunking it into the stew. "You know just what I like."

I clenched my fists under the table, her praise only making things harder.

If she were to ask me why I spent so much time holed up in my room, I'd be tempted to admit it was to get away from her before she had me throwing all caution to the wind. Did she even realize what she was doing? Sometimes, I wondered if she did it on purpose. Sometimes, I swore she *had* to be doing it on purpose.

"I'm glad you're enjoying it," I finally muttered under my breath. "I decided to try something new."

"I thought so," she mused. "It's a little bit spicy, but I like it."

I grunted again as I started eating my fill.

Focus on the food, Verus, not your tempting wife sitting across from you.

The new spice blends I'd picked up brought out the best flavors in the stew, just as the vendor had said they would. The unfamiliar taste made me think of other elemental fae and how different their food might be from ours, what variety of plants and beasts might populate the lands they lived on with their different climates.

A part of me wondered what it had been like before elemental fae lived separately and fully contained to our respective courts. No matter what the Iris said, it just didn't feel natural. But if it had been decreed by the stars, how could we question it? That would be treason. Still, it had never stopped me from imagining underwater cities far from here, where Argenti might live out from under the Iris' oppressive rule.

"Verus? Where did you go?" Ari asked, breaking me out of my musings. "I asked you a question."

"Sorry. What did you say?"

"My mother sent word that she wanted us to visit soon. Can we make something work?"

"Sure," I grunted as I tried to finish my meal quickly.

Arianwen often tried to make conversation after she finished her food, which I'd had to shut down, and I was starting to feel guilty for my rude behavior. I wasn't sure what was worse, the awkward silences or the contented moans she filled the space with. She was becoming impossible to ignore.

I didn't want to get to know and risk falling for this beautiful female sitting across from me. It felt like a betrayal to the mate I'd never see again. Was she even alive? Had she married an Iris prick? Was she being forced to bear their children? I closed my eyes briefly, the aching pain when I thought of her threatening to overwhelm me.

I stood suddenly from the table, grabbing my glass and bowl and bringing it over to be washed.

"I'm going out to meet Tal tonight," I said. "See you tomorrow."

I glanced over my shoulder and caught a glimpse of hurt and disappointment on her face. Yes, I needed to get out of here before I pulled her into my arms and tried to make her feel wanted even though I could never truly give her my heart. It was no longer mine to give.

"Okay . . ." she said quietly.

Unable to stay a moment longer, I left my dishes unwashed and headed for the mudroom. Grabbing a small bag of coin, I pushed through the water barrier and was off.

I felt somewhat bad for lying about meeting Tal, but I'd had to get out of there, and he usually hung out at one of our favorite taverns in the underwater city center. Stars willing, he'd actually be there.

I swam through the dark waters, leaving Sterling behind because I needed to clear my head. Having the cool pressure of my element around me worked wonders for my soul.

Entering the tavern, I scanned the room, looking for my friend. My shoulders drooped in disappointment when I didn't see him, but I swam up to the bar and took a seat. The tavern was half underwater with a large pocket of air at table and bar level. The room was filled with chatter and laughter as well as the soulful tune of a singer performing to a half-listening audience.

"Verus," the bartender said warmly. "I'm not used to seeing you here on a weeknight. Everything all right at home?"

"Give me your strongest ale please," I replied. "It's been one of those days."

"Sorry to hear that, lad. Hope it all works out." He poured me an amber-colored drink and set it on the table. "Are you hungry?"

I placed a coin on the bar and shook my head. "No, thanks."

The cool liquid slid down my throat, the slight burn warming my insides. As I sat savoring the feeling, the water surged slightly around me as someone swam up to my right. I looked over at the attractive female—her dark hair was loose with small shells woven in it, her skin tinted a violet hue. Her clothes clung to every curve, my eyes immediately drawn to the low-cut dress she wore, or rather to what it failed to conceal.

Faex. This is the last thing I need.

"Hey, handsome," she said with a deep and sultry voice, biting her plump lip. "Are you here all alone?" She leaned against the bar, her arms shoving her breasts together so they were even more prominent.

I glanced away from her, hoping the lack of attention would send her elsewhere.

"I'm waiting for a friend," I said coolly.

"I'm Jasmine," she crooned. "What's your name?"

"Not interested," I ground out, annoyed that she hadn't taken the hint.

She laughed brightly. "That's what they all say, but why else would you be sitting here all by yourself and away from home? Trouble with your wife? I can make you forget . . ."

She reached over, and before I could stop her, trailed her sharp nails down the front of my chest, leaving claw marks on my exposed skin. She tried to reach lower, but I grabbed her hand firmly and moved it away.

"Jasmine, I mean this in the nicest way possible, but you need to take your business elsewhere."

She put on a pout and leaned closer to me, her hand gripping my thigh under the water. "Let me know if you change your mind . . ."

She swam off in search of another victim, and I scrubbed my face. I had come here to get away from female trouble. As attractive as Jasmine was, I would never be unfaithful to my wife. I could hardly let go of the female I would never even see again . . . I was a mess.

"Verus!" a friendly voice said before slapping a hand on my shoulder. "What in the depths are you doing out tonight?"

"Tal," I said with relief. "I was hoping you might be here."

He chuckled. "I need to take advantage of all the time I have left before I'm an old married male like you. What are you doing out? Don't you have a wife at home waiting for you?"

"Yes, that's the problem," I ground out, finishing off my ale and motioning to the bartender to pour me another.

"Have you taken her to bed yet?" Tal asked quietly so no one would overhear.

He was the only friend I had who knew the truth of our situation.

I let out a dry laugh. "What do you think?"

Tal squeezed my shoulder and nodded his thanks as the bartender brought him his preferred drink. "I know you don't want to hear this, but at some point, you are going to have to let *her* go. She's not coming home, and even if some crazy, stars-damned miracle happens, you're married. You could never be with her. She would want you to find happiness."

I groaned into my hands before rubbing my temples. "I know what you're saying is true, but how in the stars do I let go of my mate?"

Tal nodded sympathetically.

"Why would the stars have given me a mate only to rip her right out of my grasp?" I asked, my voice bordering on desperation.

Tal shook his head. "Just look around, Verus. Look at our lives. Do you really think the stars care about us? At some point, you just need to move on with your life. You have a beautiful wife, you're about to be a father. Can you find a way to be grateful for that?"

"You speak a lot of truth, but it doesn't mean I have to like it," I groaned.

"That's what I'm here for," he said with a cheeky grin.

"She deserves more," I said morosely.

"Who?"

"Arianwen." I sighed loudly. "There's most definitely attraction between us. I've seen the way she looks at me when she doesn't think I'm watching. My hand and I are getting tired."

Tal groaned loudly. "Verus, you need to get laid. As soon as possible."

"It's not fair to her. If I were to take her to bed, she'd think it meant more than just a release."

"Would that be so terrible? To care for your wife? Don't you think she'd understand if you just talked to her about it?"

"I'm sure she'd love that," I groaned. "She's always trying to get more out of me, but that means making myself vulnerable . . . and if I'm being honest, I don't know if I'm ready for that, or if I'll ever be. Even though *she* isn't coming back, it still feels like disloyalty. I gave her my heart."

"That may be true, but she still went to the draft, Verus. She knew the risk she was taking staying in Iveria and that it meant you would have to move on if she were chosen. She would not want you to spend the rest of your life broken over her."

"So . . . what? I'm just supposed to tell my wife that my heart is with another so she'll never have my love, but that's all right because she can have my cock whenever she'd like it?"

Tal laughed. "I'm telling you that all you need to do is tell her the truth. Her response might surprise you."

"When we got married, we agreed to keep the past in the past. I haven't asked her about hers, and that's working."

"Is it?"

I narrowed my eyes. "To a point. I don't know. I think if I open up about my history, she might think she needs to open up about hers, and whenever she even thinks about saying something, she winces in pain. I'm telling you, if I could somehow find the person who made her swear that oath, I would so they could break it, but I wouldn't know where to start. And sometimes . . . I wonder if the male she was with, if he will come back for her and she'll leave just like—" I couldn't even say her name. It hurt too much.

Tal slung an arm over my shoulder. "I wish I knew what to tell you, but I *can* tell you that sitting here and drinking the night away is probably not the best idea considering you have to be up early tomorrow."

"You're right, absolutely right." I downed the rest of my ale. "I'll see you soon, Tal."

"Take care, Verus," he said.

Shoving through the water barrier, I couldn't hold back a yawn as I worked to siphon the water from my clothes. It had been a while since I'd been out this late, and there was a solid chance I'd be regretting my choices in the morning.

I flipped my damp hair back and stumbled past the kitchen.

Faex, perhaps I had a few too many drinks.

The lingering scent of the tavern clung to my skin despite the swim, and I wanted to scrub it off me before collapsing into bed. The door to the bathing chamber swung open, and suddenly, I was face to face with my wife.

"Verus! You startled me," she gasped as she pulled the door shut behind her.

"Apologies, wife," I said as my eyes trailed down her figure. Were her breasts bigger? They strained against the silky material she was wearing, and maybe it was the ale, but suddenly, I just wanted her. All the excuses I had been making fled as I took in the undeniable beauty of the female in front of me.

Stepping toward her, I rested my forearm on the door above her head.

"Um . . . Verus? Can I help you?"

Her breathing had gone shallow, her scent changing, and I smiled as I breathed her in. "Do you have any idea how exceptional you are? I've been trying so hard to resist you. The sounds you make and those soft, dewy lips they part from. The way you swim and the way your clothes cling to your curves . . . but I haven't even gotten to what most draws me to you. Your ability to smile when the world wants to bring you down—your resilience and your strength. Arianwen, I find myself completely enraptured by you."

I brushed her hair back from her face and slowly trailed my fingers down her cheek, her throat . . . When my fingers brushed past the soft curve of her breast, I couldn't help but notice the slight shiver that went through her body—the pebbling of her skin as she reacted to my touch.

"Verus . . ." she said breathily.

Continuing my exploration, I trailed my fingers lower, but when I got to the hem of her nightgown and started to slide my fingers up her bare thigh, she inhaled deeply, and a look of disgust came over her face.

Before I could understand what was happening, she raised both hands and shoved me away from her. She was strong for a little thing, and I stumbled back a step.

"You smell like a tavern and cheap perfume," she ground out, her eyes dropping to my chest where the telltale marks Jasmine had left were visible. A look of betrayal crossed her features, and she pushed past me, heading toward her room.

"Wife," I muttered. "It's not what you think."

"It doesn't matter."

"Please," I breathed.

Stopping at the threshold to her room, she looked back at me with cold, hurt-filled eyes. "Just stay out of my way, and I'll stay out of yours." She slammed the door shut, and I groaned.

Faex. I really had gotten myself in too deep this time.

Way to go thinking with your cock instead of your head, Verus. But perhaps this is for the best.

CHAPTER 14

UNSPOKEN WORDS

ARIANWEN

Knowing my words had been harsh, I woke up early the following morning to talk things over with Verus, but he was already gone. I sat beside the hearth alone, waiting for the water to boil. With eyes trained on the front door, I tried willing him to reappear. I hadn't meant to throw his words back at him. Tears fell unbidden as I tried to imagine a future with an absent husband. Perhaps this would forever be my curse for trying to forsake my duty all those months ago.

The tenuous peace in our home was replaced with tension and avoidance. As much as I hated the way we'd left things, perhaps it was for the best. It's what he'd wanted after all.

Verus continued to shut me out, picking up extra shifts at the shipyard and staying away from me like I might pass on some plague. The emptiness of our home had me filling every spare moment I could with work. I could no longer hide my pregnancy from the rest of my colleagues, and while Dalia was understanding, it was getting harder to avoid the onslaught of questions about family life and my future. Quilla continued sending me out to the wealthiest sections of Iveria, even with my repeated requests to work elsewhere. I had asked for no special treatment—wanting to be in the hospitium where they needed me most—but Quilla had insisted.

With my work as a healer bringing me in and out of various homes and places, I couldn't help but keep my ears open for talk of rebellion. I *knew* it existed, and the defiant part of me that had awoken on my matri-ritus had never fully returned to a peaceful slumber. If I could find them, I would find a way to help.

My most challenging house visits were to Lucris' wife, Heather. She suffered terribly from what seemed to be every possible pregnancy ailment under the stars. Her husband was unforgiving and self seeking, making everything harder on her, and I felt compelled to check in weekly to bring her tonics and emotional support.

Lucris had rubbed me the wrong way since the day I'd first stepped foot in their home. Beyond that, his business dealings seemed off—starting with bumping into him at the market so many months ago. I couldn't put my finger on it, but something felt different about him, especially with how he'd give me calculating looks whenever I showed up. I hadn't missed the way his eyes had gleamed with curiosity when he'd spotted the oath mark on my hand.

One afternoon, I stopped by earlier than expected. Raised voices filtered through the cracked doors of Lucris' office, hushing to a dead silence as I attempted to sneak past undetected. I really didn't want to be stopped or scrutinized by him again, but Lucris opened the door just wide enough to see me. Despite knowing better, I looked straight past him to see if I could catch a glimpse of who he'd been having harsh words with. I flinched backward as Lucris slammed the door in my face. I would need to be more cautious in the future.

As I continued toward Heather's room, I could have sworn I scented the deep and robust aroma of coffee brewing.

Damn the stars. They must be mocking me.

Caught between the desire to investigate the smell and my fear of Lucris catching me, self-preservation won out when I heard his voice booming from behind the closed doors. I hurried along, forcing myself to believe it was nothing more than my overactive imagination.

"Husband?" I said just as Verus was leaving for work.

"What? I'm running late," he groused.

"Thank you for making breakfast as usual . . ." I wrung my hands together. After all this time, I had finally caught him, just to find myself tongue-tied.

He shrugged, then swung his pack up and over his shoulder in that effortless way of his.

"Wait!" I followed him into the mud room.

His body froze, and he looked over his shoulder, his face impassive.

"I was thinking we could do dinner together tonight. Dalia said it would be a slow day today, so that will give me time to stop by the market and pick up some fresh fish." I stood there patiently, waiting for a response, my whole body buzzing with nerves from being so close to him in such a small space. "I feel like we haven't spoken in weeks."

"And?" He raised a brow. "Why bother pretending? There's no one here to see us."

"Please." My voice came out small.

"Have a nice day at work, Arianwen," he said before pushing through the water barrier.

I screamed curses that he would never hear. Yes, I'd said one thoughtless thing in the heat of the moment, using his own words against him. I'd been furious with him for what I assumed he'd done. I still was, but didn't we owe it to ourselves to hear each other out? Make amends?

My mind flashed back to that night. Had he meant any of the sweet things he'd said before I pushed him away? Perhaps I'd been too quick to anger. Now all I had was regret.

Almost every day, I awoke to an empty home and returned from work to more quiet. Verus did his best to avoid me at all costs, only showing signs of his presence through the breakfast and dinner he prepared and left for me. How could he be so caring yet so incredibly cold? Was he doing it out of guilt?

The rare moments I saw him, we passed each other silently in the halls. Any time I tried to speak with him, he'd make an excuse or disappear into his room to do stars knew what.

Before heading home one evening, I stopped by one of the sacred lagoons to watch the sun set over the horizon. I sat atop the craggy cliffside, opening up all of my senses to ground me, resting a hand on my swollen belly. Waves crashed upon the shore, and gulls cried out their parting songs. Soon, temperatures dropped with the sun's descent, and the stone beneath me grew cold.

The sky had darkened to a deep, dark blue when the thought occurred to me that no one would be waiting for me at home. Never before had I felt so alone, even with the babe inside me. There was an emptiness in my life that would not fill regardless of the hours I spent helping patients and distracting myself with work and studies. I couldn't help wondering if I'd made a mistake in leaving. I missed my friends in Zephyria . . . If I were being completely honest with myself, I missed *him*. But even thinking about him felt like a betrayal to Verus, in spite of our unbearable arrangement.

My saving grace—my Aella—stormed into our lives one night under a sky full of stars. I looked down at my precious baby. I counted her ten fingers and ten toes and kissed her soft little nose. Her silvery skin glimmered in the moonlight that danced off the waves of the sea. Other than the small, white, star-shaped birthmark on the back of her neck, no one would ever suspect she was only half Argenti.

As I stared into her deep blue eyes speckled with stars, I saw hints of Wynn. My heart twinged with guilt that he would never know about her. Would he have accepted and loved her, or hidden her away? In my heart, I believed he would have been a wonderful father, regardless of everything.

A slight breeze swept through my hair as my daughter stretched and yawned before rubbing at her eyes. She could never know where she'd come from. Her life would be forfeit if anyone discovered our secret. I only hoped that I could keep her safe in this world, as I couldn't imagine one without her in it.

Thank the stars Verus was such an incredible father to her, taking to parenthood as if he had been born for it. His eyes lit up every time she made a sound or gave him a smile. In some ways, she had started to bring us closer together. He came home from work earlier to spend time with her, and during long nights when she wouldn't settle, he would take her so I could sneak in a few hours of sleep.

Verus made no mention of Aella's powers. I had hoped with the lack of training, her other gift would lie dormant, but the occasional breeze that would whip around us when she fussed had confirmed my worst fears. I'd find other ways to train her—to still the little storms inside. As with anything to do with my matri-ritus, so much remained unspoken. My heart ached a little at the knowledge that I could never truly be known by anyone again.

CHAPTER 15

My Daughter

VERUS

I'd been told that parenting was hard, that it challenged even the strongest of marriages. Perhaps that would have been true if we had a typical marriage. If anything, Aella was what held us together. We were both committed to our little whirlwind.

I had never understood how a heart could grow until she came into my life. From a pit of despair and emptiness after my mate had left—it felt as if something leaped inside me every time Aella smiled or cooed. Was it possible for a heart that was ripped out to find its way back? I wasn't sure, but her big, blue eyes like saucers drew me in. She'd stare up at me like I was her whole world. I'd thought I had no heart left to give, but she tugged at strings that seemed to be stitching it back together, one small suture at a time.

For all the challenges, Aella was an easy child. She rarely cried, content to ride around in her mother's carrier for hours on end. My biggest regret was the time I lost picking up extra shifts so that I could continue to save for a nicer home above. And I hated that my wife had been working herself ragged; maybe if I provided better, she wouldn't feel she had to.

Arianwen's father had assured me my promotion was coming soon.

I just had to hold on a little longer, work a little harder, and I could give them both the life they deserved.

Aella yawned, her pudgy little arms stretching above her with hands in tightly balled fists. Half-moon eyes blinked up at me, distracting me from the subtle wind that danced around the room in greeting.

"Good morning, sweetheart," I murmured, kissing the top of her soft, fuzzy head.

The first few times I'd noticed her air element had been the most unnerving. I'd looked at Arianwen, noting her face stricken with fear—likely that I would ask a question she couldn't answer. I just added it to the list of things we would never speak of, not that we even spoke much now. Arianwen had stopped trying to draw me out. I had shut her out too many times. It was for the best.

Perhaps our little Aella was star-blessed and I would never fully understand. She was touched by them—from the mark on her neck to the stars in her eyes.

The soft sound of padding feet grabbed my attention, and I spun to see Arianwen, looking drained though the day had yet to fully start.

"Time to go to work," she said, reaching for Aella.

"Just give me one more minute with my daughter." I squeezed my little girl a bit closer. She was mine. No one could say she wasn't.

Arianwen pursed her lips. "Fine, but I really need to leave soon."

I turned my attention back to Aella and lifted her up to my face, delighted when she broke into a big, gummy smile. I could almost swear it was mine—something in the eyes, the way she mimicked me. Her silky black hair was straight as spears, and her silver skin was bright as the stars.

"Be good for Mama today," I said before pressing a kiss to her forehead.

Her little body squirmed in my arms as I carried her to the kitchen, passing her off to her mother with a quiet nod. I turned on my heel and headed to my room as I always did. It was easier to avoid the painful looks and the guilt that crept over me. I was worried that if I spent just one moment longer in Arianwen's presence, I might find myself lingering. I was so drawn to her—one moment more, and I might never leave.

Closing the door behind me, I leaned against it, my body yearning to be closer to her. Her gentle voice was muffled through the cracks as she murmured sweet nothings to our little girl. If I could have taken it all back, I would never have gone to the tavern that night, never have made such a fool of myself in front of her. Maybe things wouldn't have been so tense between us. The mere memory of it sickened me. I was so full of shame, I couldn't bear to face her again. I knew she hadn't meant what she'd said, that she'd only been throwing my own words back at me. But it was exactly what we needed—to live apart. No one would get hurt that way.

On so many occasions, Arianwen had tried to reach out to me and show her regret. She'd tried to start over—her genuine kindness and interest shining through the hurt—but I'd hardened myself to her. I saw no alternative. That night was the perfect example of what would happen if I let my walls down around her, and I just couldn't do that again.

CHAPTER 16
THE PERFECT SPY

"Good morning, Sterling," I crooned. The grumpy old seahorse gave me a sidelong glance and a half-hearted snort in acknowledgement. It could have been his fondness for the baby or the fact that I spoiled him rotten with lots of treats, but the twinkle in his eyes was proof enough that I'd finally cracked through. Deep down, I was certain he was just a big ole softie.

After securing Aella in her wrap on my back, Sterling and I took off for my next assignment. It had been a while since I'd been to Lucris and Heather's shoreline estate. Our weekly visits had come to a standstill once Heather's health had drastically improved after childbirth.

I found myself filled with both eagerness and dread once I was notified of their request to return. Their daughter, Viera, had taken ill.

A housekeeper answered the door and quickly ushered me toward the nursery. Viera was inconsolable in the arms of a nanny, the baby's dark curls plastered to her damp skin, her cheeks flushed with fever.

"Oh, sweet baby," I soothed as I carefully examined her. "How long has she been like this?"

"A few days maybe?" the nanny explained. "She hasn't been herself, cries nonstop. Nothing's working. She's like a little ball of fire, and the rash on her belly just keeps getting worse. I've tried everything. I'm not sure what else to do."

"May I see?"

The nanny carefully placed Viera into her cot, stepping out of the way. It was clear she cared dearly for the child with the way she stood watch, the dark circles under her eyes proof of the sleepless hours spent tending to her. I unraveled Viera's swaddle and peeked under the hem of her gown, surprised at the angry, raised blisters and welts on her skin. This was not something I had ever seen here in Iveria, but . . . no. It couldn't be. The last time I'd seen anything like this was when an infection had swept through Zephyria with the arrival of new refugees from Ilithania. Liisa had explained it was a common childhood illness seen in the Court of Earth, contagious and deadly if left untreated but one that responded quickly to the correct mixture of herbs and care. Without some kind of exposure, that couldn't possibly be what this was. I quickly ran through every possible alternative, but nothing else quite fit. The nanny explained the home remedies she had tried—most ineffective or even making things worse—and my mind kept going back to Zephyria. How in the stars would it have made its way *here*, into *this* home?

Aella was sleeping peacefully on my back, but there was still a risk for exposure, so I'd need to be extra cautious not to touch her. Keeping that in mind, I cleansed my hands thoroughly before opening my well-stocked pack. At the bottom, hidden beneath all of the medicinal herbs and instruments, rested my small healer's handbook from my time in Zephyria.

I ran my finger down the index in search of pox and other ulcerative maladies, and there it was, Southen Pox. Just as I'd concluded, Viera's symptoms checked all the boxes. I sighed in relief. I could treat this. I'd worry about how it got here later.

The herbs I needed for the mixture were common enough, but it was the unique combination and application that Argenti healers would have never considered. Unfortunately, though I had the right ingredients, I was missing some of the tools I needed to heat and prepare the salve. I thought about all of the nosy healers back at the hospitium and whether I'd be questioned about what I was concocting. Baby Viera's cries pinched at my heart. Perhaps if they allowed me access to their kitchen here . . . I turned back to the nanny who was wrapping the baby back up.

"Keep her unswaddled—it will help to lower her temperature. I believe I can treat her, but I'll need a few things to prepare the remedy. Is Heather available?"

"She's in her room, but . . . she hasn't come out since Viera fell ill. She believes her daughter is cursed. She . . ." Her eyes beaded with tears. "Are you sure you can help her? Have I made her condition worse by swaddling her? I promise I was only trying to comfort her. She's been in so much pain."

"It's all right. You did the right thing—you called me here."

She nodded her head with a sniff while rocking frantic baby Viera in her arms.

"I know just what to do," I reassured her. "She's very lucky to have you."

❖

Knocking gently on the door, I peeked my head into Heather's room. I caught her sitting in a chair, staring blankly out the window to the vast sea below. A tray of tea and breakfast foods sat untouched on the table beside her.

"Heather . . ." I made my way over, sitting in the chair next to hers so we could speak eye to eye. She didn't even turn her head to look at me or acknowledge my presence. "I know you're scared, and that's perfectly normal. Maybe you feel exhausted or . . . alone." The last word I found almost too difficult to utter. "Your baby, she's going to be all right. I can treat her."

She finally turned her gaze on me, eyes coming alight as emotion rushed into her face. She took a deep, shuddering breath as if returning from the dead.

"It's all my fault," she whispered.

"No, Heather."

"I wished it so. So many times . . . I wished my suffering would end. I cursed my own child." Tears rolled down her pale cheeks as she stared out the window again, falling back into that dark place.

"You know how I know that isn't true?" I asked, taking one of her hands in mine. "I saw how hard you fought during your pregnancy. Even now, you are still fighting every day. I see your struggle."

Sobs broke free, and she gripped my hand tightly. "Did you say you could help her?" she choked out.

"Yes. I can. But I need something from you."

She took some deep breaths to calm herself down. "Yes."

"You're going to need to take care of yourself. All right? She needs her mama. Promise me you'll do that for her?"

She nodded her head, and I smiled, holding back tears of my own.

"I have almost everything I need, but I really don't want to have to go all the way back to the hospitium to prepare her treatment if I can just make it here. I'll need to use the hearth—"

"Whatever you need. Use whatever you need," she said.

While I methodically prepared Viera's remedy, my heart ached for Heather and what she was going through. All this time, I'd been harboring resentment about being assigned cases with the wealthier houses in place of needier families whom I'd deemed more in-need of or deserving of care. Could I really say that Heather's needs were any less significant or any less debilitating? I'd have to make sure I found time to stop by and check on her more regularly.

I scoured the kitchen for the tools and cookware I needed, stopping when a familiar scent hit me. Holding the small, long-handled pot up to my nose, the bottom stained a deep brown, I gave it a quick sniff. Coffee had been brewed within. Unmistakably coffee.

I thought of the strange sense I'd felt in the market all those months ago.

The day I'd bumped into Lucris, just moments before that cool, pine-scented breeze had whisked past. I thought of all his strange, secretive behavior, and now Viera's illness. It was all coming together. Was he involved in the rebellion somehow and had exposed their daughter to outsiders? That was the only explanation that made sense to me.

What I couldn't wrap my head around was how Lucris, the arrogant and vindictive male that he was, could be involved in the rebellion. What he'd even have to gain from it. In his position of comfort and authority among the Argenti, it made absolutely no sense why he would risk his neck, even for a just cause. But if I wanted to find a way to join, to help, perhaps he was who I'd been looking for.

"Nosing around in the kitchen, I see." Lucris' voice startled me out of my thoughts, nearly making me jump.

I spun around to face him, the small pot still in my hands. I swallowed.

"Are you going to explain what you're doing in here?"

I cleared my throat. "I was just—uh, your daughter. I'm working on her remedy." I turned back toward the work surface and began adding the prepared ingredients into another pot, setting it over the flame. All the while, I could feel Lucris' eyes on me, scrutinizing my every move. He stepped closer, and nerves fired through me, my eyes widening at my handbook, which still lay open on the counter. To close it now would look suspicious.

"Why is it that your concoction will work when others did not?" Lucris stepped closer.

"It's an old technique I learned during my travels," I replied, picking my book up. I could just pretend I needed to find something in it.

Lucris snatched it from my hands and scoffed as he read what had been written on the pages.

"Have you been to the Court of Air?" The mere mention of it caused a searing pain. I blinked, attempting to compose myself. When I didn't answer right away, he raised his voice. "Don't make me ask you twice!"

I flinched as though struck. Lucris stared me down, intimidating me to speak. The silence tempting me to fill it with excuses and explanations. But I squeezed my hand into a fist, remembering my oath. For once, it might protect me, if it didn't kill me first.

Lucris' eyes darted toward my hand before brightening with understanding.

"You've made a star-sworn oath. Don't bother trying to hide it. I've seen your scar. Does that prevent you from speaking of it?"

Lucris was not going to stop until he got answers that satisfied him. But I wasn't going to just give up and let him corner me. I had questions for him as well.

I raised my hand showing him the mark. "I have traveled quite *far*, and I have seen this illness before and treated it successfully. The chances it could have spread here by the Iris are . . . let's just say, the odds are impossibly low. I think you know as well as I do what that means."

Lucris stepped closer, towering over me in an intimidating stance. I would not shrink back. I would hold my ground.

"What exactly are you implying?" he asked with a calculating look.

"Your daughter is sick because you've been in contact with outsiders. And if you don't let me treat her, she will die." I turned back around, attending to the fragrant concoction that currently bubbled and thickened over the flame. Almost ready.

"That's a pretty strong accusation, coming from you. You know the laws here and that I work with Lord Caelum," he threatened.

"Yes," I said over my shoulder. "Which means you have a lot farther to fall." I grabbed the pot from the flame, carefully pouring it into a small jar. "Now, if you'd excuse me, I need to go treat your daughter." I held my hand out for the handbook.

Lucris' eyes narrowed, but he handed it over. "When you are finished, I'd like to have a word with you in my study."

I gathered the rest of my things, piling them hastily into my pack, and left. I couldn't get away from him fast enough. As soon as I was out of his space, I squeezed my eyes shut, my pulse drumming in my ears. The false confidence I'd summoned only moments ago was quickly fading. This had been a mistake. I'd made a massive faexing mistake.

I peeked over my shoulder to see baby Aella was awake, her big, blue eyes taking in her surroundings. "Hey there," I sighed. "Mama's just gotta finish up here, and then we'll take some time off before my next patient. All right? Maybe we can spend a little time by the lagoon? Does that sound good to you?"

Aella cooed her response. Yes, that's what we would do.

Applying the cooling salve to poor Viera's blistered skin, I shuddered to think what would have happened if they hadn't summoned me. Perhaps the stars were on her side. Handing her back to the nanny, I gave her the jar of the concoction and instructions, urging her it was of utmost importance to keep herself and Viera away from any other children until the blisters dried and scabbed over. It would be much harder to explain my ability to cure this ailment to the Iris if it swept across Iveria the way it had in Zephyria.

Knocking on Heather's door, I peeked my head in to check on her again before leaving. To my dismay, I caught her and Lucris in the middle of a stern discussion.

"I'm so sorry to interrupt! I just wanted to let you know your daughter's fever has broken and she is resting peacefully. She should be fully recovered in a few days."

"Thank the stars," Heather murmured. "Thank you." She turned to Lucris, her eyes shimmering with unshed tears. His lack of emotional response seemed to bother her, and my distaste for the male grew stronger.

"Everything should be fine," I said in a calm, soothing voice, hoping to put her at ease. "I am going to head out now, but I'll be back in the morning to check on her. If you have any concerns overnight, please don't hesitate to send for me."

I turned to leave, hoping I could get out of another confrontation with Lucris, but I was halted at the door.

"You've been to the Court of Air, yet you returned. Did you not like the taste of freedom?"

"Iveria is my home," I said. "And I hope that one day, things might be better here, for all of us." I turned back around to leave again.

"Come back in here, Healer. This could be used to our advantage. You took an oath and cannot speak of the Adamas or Zephyria, correct?"

I flinched as pain seared my hand at the mere hint of a nod from me.

Lucris chuckled in delight. "You're the perfect spy; you cannot reveal pertinent information without great cost. I assume you know about the rebellion?"

At my lack of response, he smiled again.

"I will need to figure out how to use you. It is a challenge that you cannot speak freely to anyone, but perhaps there is a use for you yet."

Mixed feelings flooded me at this discovery. I had been looking for the rebels, but there was something about Lucris that gave me pause.

"How can I know if I can trust you? Is there anything you can tell me?" I asked hesitantly, wondering if the mark would allow me to seek information from someone else.

"Is there something specific you would like to know?" Lucris replied, a glint in his eyes.

"Who is your contact on the outside?"

He scoffed, "You overestimate your value if you think I would reveal that to you. If there is any way you can be of use, I will send for you. You'll come under the guise of healing services, and no one will be the wiser."

"Lucris, are you sure this is a good idea? She's just a healer," Heather said softly.

"I am speaking!" Lucris snapped at her. "How many times must I tell you not to cut into my conversations?"

Heather shrunk away, and his arrogance lowered my respect for him even more.

"If I am to spy for you . . . I would ask you for something in return," I spoke up, drawing his attention back to me.

"What is that?"

"If I ever need to get my family out of the Court of Water, you will see that it is taken care of."

Lucris tilted his head, his thumb and forefinger stroking his chin. "I suppose if you prove useful to me, I could owe you that favor."

"Thank you . . ." I muttered quietly. "May I go?"

He waved his hands at me dismissively, and I couldn't help but notice how withdrawn Heather had become again.

No, I did not like Lucris one bit. I wondered why the rebels would even work with him or what he was getting out of it, since he clearly didn't have a sympathetic bone in his body. Helping people escape shouldn't be used as a favor.

Knowing Wynn, he would accept any and all refugees who needed a way out—not that I had a way or was prepared to contact him. The sun would breach the darkest depths before I willingly spoke to Wynn again.

CHAPTER 17

THE MOST CONFUSING MALE IN ALL OF IVERIA

ARIANWEN

Pushing through the water barrier, I didn't even take the time to siphon the water out of my clothes and hair as I trudged through the empty kitchen and collapsed onto the sofa. My feet were swollen and aching from standing for hours on end, and I couldn't get off of them quickly enough. Aella was sound asleep in her wrap on my chest.

Something smelled delicious, but I didn't have the strength to get up to feed myself. Perhaps I would just sleep here tonight. Verus had clearly been overreacting when he'd complained about the comfort of this sofa last year.

"Wife," a low voice growled. "There is a puddle of water on the floor, and you're soaking the cushions."

Throwing up a vulgar gesture, I heard him mutter something unintelligible in response as I covered my face with an arm.

"If you care so much, you take care of it. It's just water, Verus," I groaned, refusing to look up at him, knowing I'd only see derision on his face.

"What's wrong with you?" he asked.

"It's been a long day," I muttered. "Just leave me alone."

"Fine," he growled. "At least let me put Aella to bed."

"Thank you," I said, peeking out from under my arm. Gently sliding her out of the wrap, I handed her off to Verus and closed my eyes again. After everything that had happened with Lucris and then several more emergency calls, I'd ended up working later than usual, and I didn't have the energy for one of Verus' moods. Perhaps I was being unfair, but half the time, he barely gave me any attention anyway.

A few minutes later, I heard his steps returning. I sat up on the sofa and glared at him. "What part of 'leave me alone' did you not understand?" My eyes dropped to his hands that were carrying a tray of food, and I immediately felt regret for snapping at him, especially after he had also put our daughter to bed. "Oh…"

He set the tray onto the small table next to the sofa. "You must be starving. You never eat while you work, and you need to keep up your strength."

"Thanks . . ." I mumbled softly. "I apologize for being rude. It's just been a long day, and everything hurts, especially my feet."

"I can't even begin to imagine," he said quietly. "You're working too hard. You need to take a day off."

I laughed half-heartedly. "I don't think I can. I already lost so much time right after having Aella."

"Arianwen, look at me," Verus commanded.

I finally met his eyes, surprised at what I saw. His frustration with me had melted into something else. Compassion, perhaps?

"What?"

"It won't kill you to take one day off. You need to take better care of yourself. Please eat something."

I picked up the tray and settled it over my lap, digging into the savory fish and vegetables he had prepared. "Thank you," I said again in between bites.

Verus used his power to siphon the water out of my clothes, my hair, and the sofa and floor beneath me, sending it out toward the sea. Surprised at how he was taking care of me, I almost spit out my food when he moved to the end of the sofa, gently picking up my legs and sitting down, nestling my feet in his lap.

"What are you doing?"

Ignoring my question, he gently picked up one of my feet and started massaging it with skilled fingers, the pressure perfect.

"Stars, that feels amazing," I moaned. "Who are you, and what have you done with my husband? What's going on?"

"I'm massaging your feet, obviously."

"But why?"

"You were complaining that they hurt, so I'm trying to help."

I groaned again as he worked the sore muscles. "Whatever you're doing feels incredible, so I don't want you to stop, but I don't know why you'd even bother. I honestly don't know what to expect from you. One moment, it seems that you care, then the next, you're ignoring me for days."

"You're my responsibility," he scoffed. "Of course I care about how you're doing."

"Could have fooled me," I quipped.

"Arianwen," he growled. "Just let me do this for you, unless you'd rather I stopped?" He turned his head and looked me in the eyes.

I blew out a breath. "Fine. Continue." He looked back down at my feet, moving on to the next one. "You're only the most confusing male in all of Iveria," I mumbled under my breath. His ears twitched, but he didn't respond to my mutterings.

The rest of my meal was finished in awkward silence. Verus stood and grabbed the tray, heading back toward the kitchen without another word. I wasn't sure if it was just my extreme exhaustion, but suddenly, I wanted to cry. This was not how I had envisioned my life, being married to a stranger who occasionally did kind things for me. Something had to change—I couldn't continue like this.

Stretching my arms overhead, I couldn't stop the yawn that came out of me. Tomorrow. I would try to make a change tomorrow. I was far too exhausted to try tonight. After rising from the sofa, I was pleasantly surprised at the effectiveness of Verus' massage. Perhaps he had a small healing gift within him that he didn't even know about.

I peeked into the kitchen, observing as he washed the remainder of the dishes.

"Verus."

He turned and looked over his shoulder. "Yes, wife?"

"I'll take tomorrow off if you do the same."

Confusion swept over his face. "Why in the depths would I do that?"

"If you don't, I'll just go back to work tomorrow," I retorted, hoping he'd take the bait. I was going to make this male spend time with me and try to crack him open like an oyster. I was tired of living with a stranger.

He rolled his eyes and returned to the dishes. "Fine, I'll just go in for a few hours in the morning, but you'd better be home when I get back."

"Agreed. Good night, Verus."

"Night."

One small victory.

CHAPTER 18
FORGET THE PAST

ARIANWEN

"Ari! Where's my sweet little niece?" Lani called out as she came in through the mudroom. Aella's air tantrums had been fewer and farther between, and she loved her aunt. Stars willing, nothing out of the ordinary would happen while Lani took care of her today.

"What? You didn't come to see me?" I said with a mock pout, then laughed. "She's napping. Do you want to help me bake?"

"Nope, you can handle that all on your own, sister." Leilani looked around the kitchen. "I forgot how tiny your home was—I almost missed it."

I rolled my eyes. I actually liked our little home. Verus kept saying we'd try to move to something bigger once he was promoted to shipwright, and he ignored all of my protests that we were fine where we were. Even with the contribution of my meager salary, it would take some time to save up for a bigger home.

"You're starting to sound like Aunt Rakhilit, Lani. You know Verus and I work hard."

She sighed. "I'm sorry, Ari. I just don't think I could ever live down here."

"It's a good thing I'm not in charge of your arrangement then," I teased. "One, you don't have any scandals going on, and two, you're Father's favorite—you'll be just fine."

Lani laughed, rolling her eyes. "Okay, sure. You're right. But you're lucky Verus is such a wonderful husband—not to mention dreamy. You always seem so happy together when we see you."

I turned around to pick out some ingredients and avoid lying to her face. "Yes, so happy."

An hour later, I was covered in flour and sugar, hoping my pastries wouldn't be a complete disaster. Surely some of Verus' kitchen skills must have rubbed off on me after all these months. Leilani was playing with Aella in our room while I sliced up some sea fruits and made a salad with whatever random ingredients I could find for lunch. I started thinking about what Verus and I could do together this afternoon. Despite fighting him on taking the day off, I realized I was actually looking forward to spending some time away from patients and doing something for myself. Hopefully I'd get to know my husband a little better as an added bonus.

The telltale splash of water alerted me to Verus' return, and I turned around to greet him. "Perfect. You're just in time for lunch."

Verus sniffed the air appreciatively. "What's that you're making?"

"Oh, just trying my hand at some of my mother's famous pastries," I said with a smile.

"That's brave of you."

"Oh, stop. I'm not completely useless in the kitchen," I retorted.

Verus' eyes darted toward the fire. "You might want to check on those then . . ."

"Faex!" I rushed over and pulled my pastries out of the fire before they were completely burnt. "Stars, thanks for distracting me, husband," I growled.

He laughed. "It's fine. I don't mind them a little extra crispy."

I shook my head in embarrassment and frustration. "I worked so hard on these."

Verus walked over and carefully moved the tray from my hands to the counter. "I appreciate the effort." He picked up one of the pastries and took a bite, chewing silently, his eyes never leaving mine. I raised an eyebrow as he swallowed. "They're perfect."

"Liar."

He grinned at me, and I couldn't help but smile back. He was so handsome when he smiled. I much preferred it over his usual scowl.

"Well, I'm here . . . you're here . . ." He trailed off. "Why did you want me to take off today? Did you need me to watch Aella?"

I served up a bowl of salad and handed it to him before filling my own. We sat down at the small kitchen table, him clearly waiting for a response. "My sister is actually here with Aella. I thought it might be nice for us to spend some time together. I hardly ever see you . . . and, like it or not, I'm not happy with how things have been."

His shoulders slouched as he looked down at his plate, a hint of the male underneath the facade of annoyance and irritation.

Is he unhappy with our situation as well?

Still worried a rejection was coming, I jumped in again before he could reply, speaking softly so Lani wouldn't overhear. "Am I that terrible? Is there no way we can somehow be friends?"

Verus' eyebrows lifted so high, they almost disappeared. "You think that I think you're terrible?"

"Well, not all the time . . . but the majority of the time, you can't even be bothered to speak to me. I think your smile earlier was one of the first I've seen in months."

"Surely you exaggerate. I smile," Verus said with a frown.

I couldn't help but laugh at the irony. "Verus, I know hardly anything about you, and we're raising a child together. Can you try to give me something?"

"We discussed this," he countered. "I won't ask about your past, and you won't ask about mine."

"I don't think that's enough for me . . ."

"It has to be."

I looked down at my food, loneliness and sorrow overwhelming me suddenly. A gentle hand squeezed mine, and I looked up, blinking away the sudden moisture that was trying to escape my eyes. Verus looked defeated, a sadness in his eyes that matched my own.

"Can we try to forget the past?" he asked. "Let's move forward. I'll try to smile a little more."

"Okay," I replied, my lips turning up into a sad smile. "That would be nice."

We finished our meal in companionable silence before Leilani and Aella interrupted us. Hopefully something small had shifted between us. And whether he liked it or not, I would keep fighting to get to know him better.

"So what would you like to do with the rest of our day off?" Verus asked as he tossed Aella up into the air and her giggles filled the room.

"I'd love to go for a swim, maybe explore some coves," I replied.

"Sounds riveting," Verus mocked.

"Please try to be pleasant, husband."

"Leave it to my sister to pick one of the most boring outings ever," Leilani teased.

As if remembering we weren't alone, Verus handed Aella to Leilani and stepped behind me, casually draping an arm across my chest. "You're right, Arianwen. I'd like nothing more than to spend my afternoon exploring hidden coves with my beautiful wife."

On our way out of the packed cluster of reef homes that made up our little neighborhood, Verus couldn't help himself from lending a quick hand to our elderly neighbor or tossing a drifting ball back to some rollicking teens.

People waved to us, and it felt good, like I belonged. I guess I shouldn't have been surprised to see how everyone reacted to Verus. Regardless of all our differences, he was a good male, and I respected that about him. It just stung that he seemed to smile and show kindness so easily to others while every encounter with me was filled with enough tension to part the sea.

Verus grabbed my hand, leading us away from the crowded communities that surrounded the main city.

As we swam closer to the surface, the water became more turquoise, and the sun's light shone down on us in dappled and shimmering patterns as it filtered through the wavy surface. Schools of brightly colored fish flitted below, leaving behind little dashes of light. I closed my eyes, relishing in my element's embrace, delighted to have a break from my usual duties.

As much as I found my work constantly pulling me back in, my sense of duty to my patients a heavy weight on my heart, I'd learned from Pluvia that I wouldn't make a very good healer if I couldn't learn to first take care of myself. I needed to remember that more.

Verus gripped my hand tighter. "You ready?" he asked as we approached a swift current of water. A bale of sea turtles zoomed by, along with other Argenti fae traveling in its rushing stream. I gave Verus a tight-lipped smile and a curt nod, unwilling to tell him how much I hated these things. I wasn't going to start off our day complaining, but the chance of collision was just so high, accounting for a significant number of injuries we treated in the hospitium. I squeezed my eyes shut as he pulled us into the current, and my shoulders sagged in relief at our perfectly executed capture.

"Most accidents happen closer to the city where it's more congested," he said as though reading my thoughts. "I wouldn't put you in danger. You know that, right? I've got you."

After some time riding the current far out into the Iverian Sea, I spotted a pod of balaena resting near the surface. Unable to help myself, I exited the stream and swam over to them, cooing over the new calf. The mother whistled a melodic series of calls and soft clicks in greeting and blinked a friendly, sky blue eye at me.

Verus watched from a distance before swimming up to join me. The new calf waved a fin at Verus and then attempted a breach as if to show off, making him chuckle.

"Ready to go?" he asked. "I have a few more places I'd like to show you while the sun is still out."

I nodded before sadly waving goodbye to the gentle giants. Hopefully we'd get to swim with them again another day.

Verus showed me all of the best places to forage for hidden treasures. We passed by an abundance of seaweed, and I couldn't help but stop and fill my pouch with as much as I could carry. As we explored more of the seabed, we dug through the sand together, finding other edible plants, mollusks, and sea fruits. I could only imagine what delicious concoctions Verus could come up with. Despite doing something so mundane together, I enjoyed seeing parts of Iveria I had never explored before. Verus wasn't bad company when he was trying. A spark of hope lit within—a hope I'd been unwilling to entertain—for a brighter, happier future for the two of us.

CHAPTER 19

BLUR OF PINK

ARIANWEN

Our swim had taken us pretty far from home, and the sun was starting to set when we finally came upon a small cove off one of Iveria's many islands. We walked out onto the smooth, sandy beach, allowing the water to glide off our bodies and out into the sea. The fine, coral sand glistened pink in the sun's last light. Verus' silver skin was like a canvas, reflecting the rosy hues back at me. He made himself comfortable in the soft, silky sand—the perfect spot to watch the sunset—and I ran my fingers through it after sitting down next to him. The sky was ablaze with colors, and large rocks and cliffs draped with lush, flowering vines surrounded the cove, creating a secluded haven just for the two of us.

"This place is gorgeous," I said. "Thank you for sharing it with me." I opened my pouch and pulled out some fruit, handing him one. "Also, thank you for making me take a day off. I really needed this."

"You and me both."

We sat in silence for a while, soaking in the peace and beauty of the cove. I couldn't help but find myself enchanted by the floral perfume from the hanging foliage at our backs and the pristine water that glistened in front of us, lapping gently against the coral shore.

"I guess it's okay to take some time off every now and then," Verus mused.

"I hate to admit how good it feels to be out here with our element," I confessed. "No expectations or urgent requests from anyone. Don't get me wrong, I love my work and what I'm able to do for people, but it's good to get away from it to remember what life is like outside of all that pain." I squeezed my knees to my chest. "It's all too easy to wind up in a dark place when you witness so much suffering."

Verus looked over at me and frowned. "You give so much of yourself, and yet you're always smiling. I don't think I realized just how emotionally taxing it was."

"Maybe it's a coping mechanism," I huffed.

"Tell me. What's been going on?"

"Quilla and Dalia have kind of thrown me into the depths with some of the hardest cases as of late. They want me to learn as much as I can, but part of the work we do is recognizing when it's out of our hands. And I don't know if I will ever get used to that. Sometimes I wonder if I'm too sensitive for this kind of work."

"If you ask me, I think that's a sign you're truly meant for it. The world needs more healers with a heart like yours." He reached over and placed a warm hand on mine, sending a shiver down my spine. "I'm sorry I haven't been there to listen."

I shrugged. "How could you have known? As I said, we barely ever talk."

Verus winced. "I'm sorry, Arianwen. You shouldn't have to carry all of that on your own. I will try to do better."

"Thank you. That means a lot."

"We're very similar: driven, hardworking . . . a little too hard on ourselves. I think we could both use a little more self-compassion."

He squeezed my hand again and let go, tearing off another piece of fruit and popping it into his mouth. I caught myself staring at his full lips, wishing for a moment that I could trade places with that fruit. My mind wandered, and I started to imagine pushing him down onto the sand and crawling on top of his magnificent body. What I wouldn't have given to run my fingers and tongue all over the beautiful markings on his chest.

Ari, what is wrong with you? What kind of fruit are you eating?

I squeezed my eyes shut and my thighs together, trying to block out the images I'd conjured in my mind. Stars, my loneliness must have been getting the better of me. Verus would surely have laughed if I'd tried to do anything of the sort.

"We should probably head home," I blurted out. "Tomorrow we'll have to go back to reality."

Verus nodded in agreement. "I'll admit, I wasn't sure I would be able to relax knowing I should be working, but it wasn't that bad."

"I'm glad my company wasn't too horrible," I said, my tone dripping with sarcasm.

A slight frown crinkled his forehead. "We should make a point of coming out here more often. But under one condition."

I perked up a brow.

"I don't ever want to hear you talking down about my wife again," he teased. "No one talks badly about my wife." He winked, then jogged off toward the sea. I caught myself sighing at his ruggedly handsome good looks, enhanced by the flirty quirk of his lips when he'd smiled, his muscles defined by cast shadows of the fading sun . . . then I had to snap myself out of it.

"Are you coming?" he called out, his brows furrowed and face twisted into a frown.

"Of course," I called back, playfully rolling my eyes at his impatience.

As I waded out into the water, I couldn't help but wonder who had wounded him so much that he was so unwilling to open up. Regardless of how much pain Wynn's actions had caused, I knew I couldn't dwell on it forever. Bitterness and anger toward him would only harm me in the long run. Seeing Verus holding on to whatever it was that had hurt him made me realize how easily I could have been there too. It made me grateful for the distraction of my work and having a purpose beyond my own pain.

The closer to central Iveria we got, the busier and more congested the waters became. This time of day, the current was filled with Argenti on their various commutes, their silvery skin shimmering like iridescent fish scales as they flitted past. Verus sensed my unease and cocooned me in his broad arms. It felt nice to be cared for and protected. Even with how much our marriage had felt like two strangers sharing a home, he'd picked up on things, intuiting my needs—sacrificing his seahorse for me, cooking and preparing meals for me, and now this. There was something comforting in the idea that he cared more than he'd been willing to let on. A lightness filled my chest, making me feel like smiling was easier and that maybe the idea of allowing myself to care for him wasn't the worst thing that could happen.

True to his word, Verus found a safe and less crowded area to disembark from the rapidly flowing current—regardless of the longer swim home it would require. This decision, which some would deem overly cautious, he'd chosen to protect me, correctly inferring how I felt about the potential of traumatic collisions. I was preparing to thank him for his consideration, but before I had a chance, he swam off, distancing himself from me again.

The underwater city flickered with the soft green glow of lights from people's windows and children chasing schools of brightly colored glow fish. It was so different from how I'd once imagined my future, but the sight of my new home filled me with a deep sense of pride and belonging.

Verus slowed down once he noticed I wasn't right behind him.

"Forgot how to swim?" he teased.

I rolled my eyes dramatically, then jetted past him, showing off a little.

"This way, sailfish. I want to make a quick detour into the city center before we head home," he said.

The underwater markets were lively this time of evening, the work-ing class stopping by to pick up fresh fish and other needs on their way home. Fish swam in circles, contained within spacious, flexible, netlike structures of miniature water currents that the fishmongers manipulated to surround and corral the fish. It always fascinated me, the sight of their fluid, near-invisible nets. Verus greeted a fishmonger by name, and I let my mind wander as he bartered for the best deals.

Most stalls remained submerged, while a few maintained water barriers to keep their wares dry. At first, I'd been a bit overwhelmed coming to these markets, which were stacked a good five to six layers high, stalls practically overlapping each other. I'd tried to make sense of the market's organization, but there was none. I couldn't just swim through it down one path like the shops up above—it would take two seconds to lose someone here.

But I was beginning to see why Verus preferred the underwater markets to the ones above, as there were usually less Iris below. All of the Iris stationed in Iveria were gifted with a water element so they could monitor the beneath, but it was rarer to come upon them.

One stall over, handwoven baskets floated on a gentle current, looped along a rope that kept them from drifting away. A group of elderly females skillfully twined strands of seaweed into various shapes and sizes, luring not only buyers but onlookers curious to see the craft. Colorful fabrics on one of the dry platforms further down snagged my attention, then I found myself drifting toward the melancholic tune of a market performer fluting music through a conch shell. Verus nudged me with his arm, breaking me out of my perusal of our surroundings.

"Were your deals favorable?" I chirped, reminding myself of my mother, and I made a mental note never to ask that question again.

"He drives a tough bargain . . . but, this fish is worth every last coin. You'll see." He smirked. "Did you need anything before we head back?"

"Hmm, I always thought I'd take up spearfishing!" I said as we passed by a shop with a variety of fishing tools.

Verus hoisted one, giving it a good spin, testing the weight hand-to-hand, then put it back and selected another. He held it up to me with a raised brow before digging through and pulling out another.

"Ah, this looks about right!" He handed me a tiny little spear with a dull tip, the size one might give a child to practice with.

I squinted my eyes at him, then bit my lip to suppress my sincere amusement.

"Spearfishing aside, I think it might be helpful to learn how to defend myself." I moved my body into a defensive posture with the tiny spear, throwing a couple of quick jabs for fun.

Verus chuckled, easily snatching it out of my hand. "What in the depths do you need to protect yourself from?" He puffed up his chest. "I'll keep you safe," he said with a wink.

I rolled my eyes at him but couldn't hold back a grin. "There are dangerous creatures in the sea as well as above. You never know . . ." I trailed off as my mind flashed to the warg I'd encountered in the woods and how helpless I had felt.

Verus frowned and opened his mouth as if he was going to ask a question, but he changed his mind. He still hadn't asked about my past. It was in the dumb agreement we'd made. I sighed, watching as he placed the spear back with the others.

Turning toward me, he tilted his head. "If you'd like, perhaps I can show you a few defensive ways to use our element."

A smile tugged at my lips, and I nodded. "I'd like that."

We passed other shops until we reached the outer stretch of the market. There was a seahorse auction, and crowds were gathered to witness the sales of the majestic creatures.

"Excuse me, miss. Would you like to buy a seashell?" A small girl tugged on my skirt.

My heart stung when I noticed her tattered clothes and unkempt appearance. I found myself speechless. She held out a simple, scalloped shell, then opened the mesh bag toward me.

"Have a look. I have blue ones, purple ones."

"They are very pretty," I said, glancing around the area. "Are you alone? Where is your mother?"

"I found them myself, I swear! I didn't steal them." The girl pulled back defensively.

"Of course not. Here, let me have a look." I glanced at Verus, unsure what to do.

Verus inclined his head. "That looks like a good one, perfect for Aella to teethe on," he nodded at the simple, white, scalloped shell in my hand.

Verus handed over the large fish he'd just bargained all his coin for, and the girl's wan face cracked with the biggest smile.

"Will this be enough?" he asked.

"That will feed my whole family! Thank you, sir! Thank you! Stars bless you!" The girl bowed her head to us then swam from the market in a hurry as though afraid she might be accused of stealing it.

Emotion welled up inside me at the gesture.

Verus took note, wrapping an arm around me and squeezing. "Don't be sad, wife," he murmured against my hair. "I'll still make you dinner. As a matter of fact, I make a mean seaweed stew."

I chuckled while shoving him gently for his teasing remark. In spite of his often cold exterior, a kind and loving heart was hidden beneath, never more evident than in his willingness to help others.

Suddenly, a blur of pink raced by, and Verus tugged me back toward him, shielding me from the seahorse's wake. I looked up at him in confusion, and he shook his head, just as stunned as I was. Within seconds, two Iris sped past, chasing after it. One of them snapped out a bloodstained coil of braided seagrass, and it caught the seahorse around the neck, jerking it to a stop. I cried out, watching as the poor creature's eyes bugged out of its head, the whip digging into its scaled flesh.

Anger bubbled up inside me at the seahorse's treatment, my healer instincts moving me to rush over and help it. Verus swam in front of me, gripping both arms and shaking his head.

He let go and said, "I know you feel you need to help, but there's nothing we can do. We can't get involved."

I gritted my teeth, barely holding back a growl of frustration.

"They won't let you near it. Just think of the potential consequences. We have too much to lose."

I glared at him, pursing my lips, hating that he was right. My eyes darted back to the pink seahorse.

I watched as the Iris caught up to it, barely loosening the whip before kicking its side. I flinched as they abused the poor creature, feeling every attack tear me up a little more inside. One of them jumped onto its back, the seahorse bucking wildly, trying to throw him off only to be stung with a whip once again. That was no way to treat any creature and only served to remind me of poor Marwen being handled the same way months earlier. The Iris clearly believed us all to be beneath them.

If that was how they treated us here in our own environment, I shuddered to think what awaited the poor souls drafted into the highly esteemed Matri-Ludus competitions. Based on what I'd learned in Zephyria and Wynn's implications, it wasn't the great honor they liked us to believe.

Once in control of the seahorse, the Iris headed back toward us. Blood inked the water from the seahorse's wounds, and the vicious guards shoved the horse in the direction of the auctioneer.

"Find me another!" one shouted. "She's a useless beast who doesn't know a master when she sees one."

The auctioneer, horrified at what shape they'd returned the seahorse in, trembled slightly. "She's the best we have . . ." he stammered, knowing well not to argue with the Iris and that they could potentially go through every last seahorse in his possession if they felt like it. The Iris guards sneered then yanked on the reins that dug tightly into the seahorse's flesh, dragging it behind them.

"Come, wife. We should get going . . . Better not let them catch us staring."

Trying to be inconspicuous, I kept an eye on the direction they were going. It wasn't that much farther when I saw them drag the seahorse into an underwater stable attached to a guard station. My heart broke—there had to be something we could do.

Verus slowed his swim when he noticed me lagging behind, and he took my hand in his. "You're not going to be able to let this go, are you," he stated.

I shook my head no, letting him see the pain it caused me.

"Let's go home and talk this over."

CHAPTER 20
THE HEIST

JRIANWEN

The minute we made it through the water barrier, I turned to him and said, "Verus, we have to go back for her. She won't survive that kind of treatment!"

"I hear what you're saying, but do you know how dangerous that sounds?" he asked. Verus quickly sent all the excess water back into the sea before walking toward the kitchen with everything we'd foraged.

Trailing after him, I continued, "I know it's dangerous, but the Iris can't get away with that."

I wrung my hands together, pacing while Verus started to put away the food. Something about the seahorse called to me, and I couldn't let her go.

"What's all the commotion?" Leilani said, and I immediately swept Aella into my arms, covering her in kisses.

"Mama missed you, sweetheart," I crooned as she snuggled into my arms.

"Well?" Lani asked, looking so much like me with her hand on her hip.

Verus snorted as he continued putting things away. "Go ahead and tell her. This is all you, wife."

"The Iris were abusing a beautiful seahorse," I replied. "I was telling

Verus that we have to do something. Do you think you could stay longer? Verus could escort you home later."

Lani's eyes widened. "You know I would help you with anything, but are you sure about this? Defying the Iris . . . it sounds dangerous."

Verus turned around to face me, leaning back against the counter and crossing his arms. "What *did* you have in mind, Arianwen?"

Not expecting that response, my mouth dropped open in shock. Was he actually willing to go along with this? A flood of warmth filled me at the thought, and a smile curled my lips. "We're going to steal her right out from under their noses."

Lani gasped, covering her mouth while Verus' eyes widened and he let out a forced laugh. "I'm not sure how you think we're going to accomplish that, but let's eat first and try to come up with a plan."

"You're not just going to say no?"

He shrugged. "I can see this is important to you, and as long as you don't try to do it alone . . . The Iris are a bunch of pricks and deserve to lose the creature with how they're treating it." He turned back to the counter and started chopping up seaweed.

"Whatever has gotten into you, Verus?"

"I'm not quite sure, Arianwen. Apparently you're bringing out the rebellious side of me tonight."

"She's clearly got you wrapped around her finger," Lani teased. "Maybe I was wrong when I thought you were boring, Ari."

I laughed. "What better way to end this day together than by stealing from the Iris."

Verus suddenly stopped, turning to me, a sliver of fear showing in his eyes. "You have to promise me something, wife."

"Yes, husband?" I fluttered my lashes at him ever so sweetly.

"If, at any time, I tell you to swim, you need to get out of there. Your life is not worth the risk. We have a daughter to think about."

Overcome with sudden emotion, I swallowed hard and kissed Aella's soft head again. "Understood."

A few hours passed as we came up with a plan to rescue the seahorse. Leilani thought we were absolutely ridiculous for even thinking about going through with it. I wouldn't say it was one of my most brilliant plans, but one could only hope the Iris wouldn't catch on and their pride would get the better of them. Who would dare steal something from our star-sent rulers after all?

Clothing ourselves from head to toe in dark attire, we crept out of our cozy home. Down below, the waters were incredibly dark during the depths of night, and despite their gifts, the Iris could not see as well as us in the murky water. Our plan hinged on the assumption that the stables would not be well guarded in the middle of the night when most Argenti would be asleep.

Verus and I had debated whether we should bring his seahorse with us for a quicker getaway. I had argued that Sterling's distinctive blue and orange coloring would too easily lead back to us if we were seen. Without the seahorse, we could hide in the dark shadows and wait for any pursuit to pass. The real question was: what would we do if we succeeded? It couldn't possibly be safe to bring her home, could it? One step at a time.

The waters were empty as we silently swam toward the Iris guardhouse on the outskirts of the city center. Built into one of the cliffs, it housed a garrison of lower-ranking Iris and reached many levels above the water. Even with their water gifts, most Iris did not enjoy living below. They claimed they needed to be closer to the stars, but I knew the truth behind those lies.

Trying to stick to the shadows, Verus and I approached the guardhouse. A few lights shone out of the windows, and there were two guards stationed at the entrance, surrounded by a small bubble of air. Faex. There was no way we could sneak out a light pink seahorse with them there. But the stables were dark, and the least I could do was check on her.

The entrance to the stables was in sight of the Iris guards, so we silently swam to the side, looking for another way in. The stables had small, barred windows. I peered inside, and when I didn't see any guards, I began tugging on the bars, hoping to loosen them somehow. While I wasn't exactly weak, they wouldn't budge.

Strong arms surrounded me from behind, gripping the bars right alongside my hands. Bracing myself with my feet on the wall and Verus' chest behind me, I continued tugging, feeling his body tense and muscles flex as he strained to loosen them with me. The wall around the window started to crumble, and hope blazed anew. Perhaps we could actually do this.

The sudden whinny of seahorses inside the stables broke through the silence of the night, and Verus and I froze. If the Iris remained in their bubble of air, the chances of them hearing us were slim, but if they had anyone stationed within the stable, we were in trouble.

Turning to face Verus, I suddenly remembered how close we were with his arms surrounding me, our faces only inches apart. His eyes glistened in the dark, a look of worry in them.

I whispered, "I'm starting to think this might have been a terrible idea."

Verus' lips twitched with amusement. "Starting to? I could have told you that from the beginning."

"Do you think we can remove the bars?" I asked quietly.

He reached around me and gave them another small tug. "Yes, but it won't be quiet."

"No one has shown up yet," I said. "I don't think anyone's inside."

"Let me check to see if the guards have moved," he whispered, then darted off to the corner of the building and peeked around the side. "We're all clear," he said. "Maybe the stars are with us—they look half asleep."

Verus positioned himself behind me once again, and with a few strong tugs, the wall crumbled and the bars loosened completely. At the sudden lack of resistance, my body was thrown into Verus. He let go of the bars, and they floated down to the seabed, his arms wrapping around me to keep me upright.

In all my excitement about our small victory, I turned and threw my arms around him, wrapping him in a hug. Our bodies molded together perfectly, and for just a moment, I let myself imagine Verus being my safe haven.

Pulling away from him, I smiled sheepishly and said, "I'm going to go look for the seahorse. Keep an eye out for the Iris?"

He nodded, and I slipped through the opening, grateful for my smaller frame. Verus' broad shoulders would have never made it through the window, regardless of the damage we'd done to it.

The stables were dark, and the soft sound of whinnies broke through. If how they treated the poor pink seahorse was any indication, the Iris did not deserve to be the caretakers of any of these creatures. I peeked into all the stalls, looking for the telltale color. Most of the seahorses were asleep.

After passing two pink seahorses that were not the one I was looking for, I started to give up hope until I reached the last stall. Gently unhooking the door, I swam in and tried to calmly approach the creature. She was barely conscious, blood oozing from the wounds around her neck. She was tied up to a post, a muzzle over her snout.

Placing a soothing hand onto her neck, I let some of my healing power flow into her. Once I had stabilized her, I gently unwound the seagrass rope from her neck. She quivered in fear, shying away from me.

"It's all right, beautiful girl," I cooed. "I promise I won't hurt you."

When I was sure she would not try to bite my hand off, I carefully removed the muzzle. I had a small pouch of seaweed wraps in my pocket and was grateful when she let me dress her wounds. My magic continued probing, and I was relieved no permanent damage had been done. How in the stars was I going to get her out of here?

An idea came to me, and I gently patted the seahorse on the nose, pulling out a small prawn I had saved in another pocket. She slurped it out of my hand, and I instantly knew I had made a friend for life.

"I'll be right back, sweet girl," I said softly, then latched the door to the stable and swam back over to the window.

Verus looked tense and startled when I whispered, "Psst. I have an idea."

Getting closer to the window, he arched a brow.

"I'm going to create a distraction."

"Stars help us," he muttered.

"Just make sure you stay away from the entrance," I replied, then swam away before he could argue.

My idea was foolish at best, but if I could time this properly, perhaps I could get away with it. Swimming up to the front doors, I looked around for something, anything, to lift the latch on the outside of the doors. My eyes caught on a thin piece of driftwood that I thought just might fit through the slim opening. I thanked the stars as it slid in perfectly and allowed me to unhook the latch holding the doors shut.

Here's hoping a stray current doesn't push them open before it's time.

I started unlatching all of the stalls as quietly as I could, making my way back toward the injured pink seahorse.

When I entered her stall, she swam up to me, nudging me as if asking for another treat. "If we get out of here, girl, I promise there are more where that came from." She nickered quietly, and I gave her nose a gentle pat. "Wait here for just a moment," I said softly, hoping she would understand me.

I swam out of her stall and back toward the broken window.

"Here goes nothing," I mumbled.

Lifting my fingers to my mouth, I let out a shrill, high-pitched whistle. The sounds of whinnying seahorses filled the stable along with the sound of doors swinging open. My heart pounded in my chest as a dozen seahorses made a break for the exit and burst through the stable doors. When a third blur of pink bolted past, I smiled, glad she had not stayed in her stall.

I pulled myself through the small opening of the window, and Verus gripped my hand, dragging me along with him. "You're either brilliant or foolish," he said with gritted teeth as we dove down deep while skirting along the side of the building.

I peeked my head around the corner and watched as a herd of seahorses exited the stable and the two Iris guards jumped to attention, diving through their pocket of air, looking surprised and angry at the disturbance. I couldn't help the small chuckle that escaped me as all of their seahorses fled into the dark waters, their speed unmatched by the unprepared Iris.

Verus pulled me behind another building, placing a hand over my mouth. I glared at him in the dark. He shrugged, moving his hand to hold a finger to his lips, as if I wouldn't know to be quiet. I rolled my eyes at him, and he leaned in close, whispering in my ear, "You were giggling only moments ago. I had to make sure you'd be quiet and not lead the Iris straight to us."

I tensed as I realized once again how close we were to each other. We waited a few minutes in silence, the shouts of the Iris fading as they chased after the escaped seahorses.

"Let's go home," Verus finally said quietly, pulling away from me.

"Thank you for helping me rescue her," I said sincerely.

The hint of a smile graced his lips before he turned and started swimming back toward our little home. I was grateful the seahorses had gotten away. Hopefully, the Iris wouldn't be able to catch any of them. I knew that, ultimately, I couldn't stop them from ever hurting another creature again, but in the very least, I had freed some.

Verus and I were swimming in silence when a blur of pink suddenly flashed through the dark waters.

No. It couldn't be.

I stopped, let out a soft whistle, and the brightly colored seahorse turned and swam straight toward me. I couldn't keep the giant grin off my face as she swam in a circle around us, sizing Verus up.

"It's all right," I crooned. "He won't hurt you." I pulled out another prawn from my pocket and held it out as a peace offering. "I'm so sorry if I scared you earlier, but I needed to get you away from there."

She approached us and swiftly stole the prawn right out of my hand.

"Arianwen, we need to get out here before she draws attention to us," Verus said calmly.

"Can we bring her with us?" I asked, willing to beg if needed.

Verus sighed and nodded, and I motioned for the seahorse to follow us if she was willing. I wouldn't force her to come with us, but it seemed I had definitely won her over.

Verus kept checking over his shoulder to see if anyone was following us, but we made it back safely without any interference. I guided the pink seahorse into our small stable, grateful there was room enough for two. Sterling looked a bit annoyed at the intrusion but whinnied softly in acceptance of the female.

"I think I'll call you Stella."

CHAPTER 21
CRUSHED SILVER PETALS

I missed my wife. Those had been the last feelings I would have ever expected, but she had been growing on me. After our day together the week prior and our daring rescue of Stella, I'd started to realize, when I stopped fighting with myself, that I actually enjoyed spending time with her, and perhaps it wouldn't have been so terrible to do it again. Preferably without putting our lives in danger and stealing from the Iris though.

We had become a little family, the three of us, but I'd hardly seen Arianwen or Aella in the previous few days. Her job at the hospitium had her working later and later every day. It couldn't possibly be good for her or Aella to be spending so much time out. I really needed to talk to her about trying to cut back some of the hours. Perhaps it was selfish, but it would be nice to see more of my daughter when she was awake.

"Lev, would you mind if I took off a little early today?" I asked. My work was mostly done for the day, and we had a lot of new recruits who had helped with the bulk of the day's labor. When he didn't respond right away, I added, "I'd like to pick up Arianwen and Aella from the hospitium and maybe go eat together. She's been working so hard."

Lev finally looked up from his work, a far-off look in his eyes. "I suppose that would be fine, as long as you're caught up tomorrow. Tell Arianwen to bring my granddaughter by for a visit soon."

"Yes, sir," I replied, unable to stop the smile stretching my cheeks wide.

I packed up my things and started making my way from the docks to the crowded city center. I felt lighter than I had in a long time, hopeful, perhaps. We could make a good life together. Our friendship, despite its rocky beginnings, was growing into something more, something that filled me with a strange kernel of sensation in my chest I wasn't yet sure how to label. Perhaps it wouldn't be the life I had imagined for myself, but the stars had a way of laughing at our plans.

A flower vendor was packing up his cart, and I couldn't help stopping to pick out a few long-stemmed flowers with dewey, silver petals, just like her eyes. It was a bit frivolous, but for some reason, I didn't want to show up empty-handed. Tal would have laughed and made fun of me for this if he knew. I wasn't sure if she would want to see me, but hadn't she been trying to spend more time with me the previous week?

The hospitium came into view, and my heart rate picked up. I had never visited her at work before.

As I approached the entrance in a brisk jog, my foot caught on a loose stone, making me nearly trip. I cursed as the flowers went flying. As I bent down to pick them up, I noticed a dispute down a narrow alley beside the hospitium.

The familiar-sounding hushed but angry voices grabbed my attention, making me turn to inconspicuously glance their way.

Sure enough, Ari stood facing off with an irate Argenti male while trying to shush a fussing Aella in her arms. My first instinct was to march over there and intervene, get that male away from her and our child, but I stopped myself. The last thing I wanted was for her to think I was being overbearing or that I thought she couldn't hold her own.

Quickly stepping out of view, I debated whether I should listen to their private conversation, but my curiosity got the better of me.

I need to know if she's in danger. It would be irresponsible not to listen in . . .

"I don't know if I feel comfortable doing what you're asking me to do, Lucris," Arianwen said, her voice filled with concern.

"Need I remind you that you're the one who wanted to get involved?" he asked, sounding irritated. "If you want me to make good on that favor to get you out of the Court of Water, you will do what I ask."

Get her out of the Court of Water? What in the depths?

I couldn't even hear the rest of the conversation as those words played over and over in my head. My wife was planning on leaving? I thought things were getting better between us . . . Had it all been an act?

Something cracked in my chest, feelings of betrayal and devastation washing over me. Crushing the flowers in my hand, I let them fall to the ground as I turned and headed back to the sea. I had been a fool to even think about letting her in. I had been a fool to let myself get attached.

CHAPTER 22

THE BARGAIN

ARIANWEN

Verus wasn't home when I returned from my shift at the hospitium.

That's odd. He always beats me home, especially now that we have two seahorses.

I hadn't seen him in two days, as he had been in bed when I'd arrived home the night before. Maybe he'd decided to go spend time with Tal, but that hadn't happened in the middle of the week since that one night I didn't want to think of.

Perhaps it made me a terrible wife, but I was more irritated that I'd have to cook for myself after a long, hard day of healing than concerned about his whereabouts.

Great job, Ari. You're utterly spoiled.

After putting Aella to bed, I busied myself in the kitchen and started preparing some food. I rummaged around, looking for the quickest possible meal option, as I just wanted to eat and go to bed. It didn't even need to be hot.

My ears perked up at the sound of shuffling footsteps followed by a groan. I turned my head and gasped at the sight of Verus, beaten and bloodstained.

"Faex! Verus, what in the depths happened to you?" I cried out. I rushed over to him, but he shoved past me, heading toward his room.

"I don't want to talk about it, Arianwen. I'm going to bed."

"You've lost your stars-damned mind if you think I'm going to let you go to bed without making sure you're all right."

He stopped and turned to me, anger burning through his eyes. "I'm fine," he growled. "I don't need anything from you."

I stepped back as if struck. I'd started to hope things were getting better between us, but his words cut like a knife. Either way, I wasn't going to let him suffer when I could do something to help. We stared each other down until he finally sighed and broke eye contact, leaning his head against the wall.

"I'm going to lie down," he rasped, and then he groaned as he straightened and started back toward the bedroom.

Rushing to his side, I looped my arm around his waist, noting how he hissed as I touched his side.

"I'm sorry. I didn't mean to make it worse."

He groaned a response as he allowed me to help him limp to the bedroom. While we walked, I subtly probed with my magic, picking up on the bruising injuries that mottled his flesh—from dislocated ribs to the pain radiating behind his ear. I had no idea how he was still standing and found myself thanking the stars that he had actually made it home. This had the Iris written all over it.

I helped him to his bed, and he lay back carefully, tensing up in pain. Flooding his body with my healing power, I saw the tension in his brow ease as some of the pain was numbed.

"You've been working all day; don't waste too much of your source power on me," he said through gritted teeth.

"I am more than capable of knowing my limits," I scoffed as I continued working, trying to focus on the most critical injuries first. I was exhausted, but he needed me, and I wasn't going to let him suffer. "What happened, Verus?"

Each breath was accompanied by a grimace, and he flinched as my hand touched a sensitive spot on his side. "I made a mistake . . . and I'm sorry, but you and Aella will pay for it too."

"What? What are you talking about?"

"The Iris," he spat out. "A rotation of guards came by the shipyard today. They're newly in from Prisma and acted like they had something to prove." He took a deep breath, wincing briefly as he tried to conceal his pain from me. "They were going after one of our newer dock workers. He must be sixteen or seventeen, but he was so nervous with the Iris there that he dropped some materials. It wasn't a big deal, but when they started threatening him, I had to do something."

"Faex," I said softly under my breath. "You didn't."

"I merely asked them to let me handle the situation, but the Iris didn't like me interfering. Said I was 'impeding their right to enforce consequences.' They almost killed the poor kid," Verus groaned out. "One of them had their hand around his throat . . . too long . . . He had stopped fighting back, but they wouldn't quit. If I hadn't stepped in . . ."

"Monsters," I spat.

"But, stars, Verus, how did you get away? Will they keep coming after you? Do they know where we live? What did you mean when you said Aella and I will pay for it too?"

"I had to make a bargain."

I briefly closed my eyes. Fear like an icy chill slid down my spine. "What did you give them?" I asked softly.

Unable to look at me, he turned his gaze to the small window. "I had to allow the beating and not fight back," he replied, his voice full of shame. "And . . . all the hard work I have done to rise up in station, to become a shipwright alongside your father . . . that's over."

"What do you mean?" My hands stilled on his broken body.

"I can never be anything more than I am. I can't give you the life you were used to. We will be stuck here beneath for the rest of our lives."

I heaved a huge sigh of relief. "Oh, Verus . . . Is that all? I don't care about any of that. I'm just happy you're alive, you're safe, and they aren't coming after you. Nothing else matters." Verus closed his eyes, and I reached over, turning his face toward mine. "Look at me," I pleaded. He blinked, one of his eyes starting to swell, and I sent more healing power into him. "I am proud of you for standing up for what you believe in, no matter the cost. I'd much rather live in the deepest, darkest depths than with a wealthy male with no honor."

Verus' eyes were filled with emotion, and he blinked as if fighting back tears. "You really mean that?" he replied, his voice gravelly.

"Yes, I really do." Our gazes were locked on each other's, and I gently brushed a stray tendril of hair off his face. He relaxed under my touch, and I smiled shyly. "You're such a papa goose."

His forehead wrinkled as he raised his eyebrows. "What did you just call me? You've said it before."

"You're like a papa goose—you're always taking care of us . . . of me. Now let me take care of you. I have just the thing to help you sleep so your body can do the rest of the healing. I'll be right back."

Before I could stand, Verus suddenly brought his hand to the back of my neck, digging his fingers into my hair, pulling me closer. He pressed his lips to mine in a surprising kiss. His lips were soft and warm, invoking a feeling of coming home that I wanted to sink into. All too soon, he pulled away and let go of my neck, murmuring a soft "thank you."

Utterly shocked and confused by the unforeseen kiss, I stood up and hurried toward the kitchen, feeling his eyes on me as I left the room. Once I was out of sight, I leaned against the wall, closing my eyes, my fingers rising unbidden to touch my lips.

Did that just happen? Did my husband actually kiss me?

A wave of emotions crested over me as I fought the conflicting feelings of desire and hesitation. For so long, he had kept me at arm's length, treated me as if I were merely a nuisance, with the exception of rare moments when I'd thought he might let me in.

Could things possibly change between us this time?

Not wanting to keep him waiting, I grabbed the herbs I needed and put together the pain-relieving tonic. While it wouldn't taste amazing, it would help stave off any lingering pain and let him rest. Once I returned to his room, I was surprised but grateful his pain had already subsided enough to allow him to fall asleep. A tiny part of me was disappointed I couldn't ask him about that kiss. It had shaken me, and I couldn't help but wonder what he'd been thinking and if he would have said or done anything else.

Wondering if I should disturb him, I hesitated but then decided he'd feel a lot better in the morning if I poured a little more healing source into him. I moved silently toward his bed and set the tonic on the small table next to it. My fingers lightly traced his face and head, infusing him with the last bits of source I had to spare, then I covered him up with one of his blankets.

I leaned down, pressed a soft kiss to his head, and whispered, "Rest well. Good night, husband."

I checked on him several times throughout the first half of the night, worry keeping me awake. Each time, I found him asleep. I was relieved once I saw he'd drunk the tonic, and I finally collapsed into my bed from sheer exhaustion, not waking again until morning.

I knocked on Verus' door, wanting to check on how he was healing.

"Come in," a gruff voice replied.

I opened the door and peeked my head in, seeing him sitting up shirtless in bed, his chest and sides dappled in dark bruises.

"How are you feeling?" I asked as I widened the door and stepped into the room.

"Everything hurts," he groaned. "I don't know if I can make it to work today."

I barked out a laugh as I leaned over him, the healer in me taking over as I quickly sent my magic into him, checking on the state of his injuries. "You're not to leave this house until I allow it. Healer's orders." I stood over him, pleased with the progress he had made overnight. "You'll probably be sore for a few days, but I do think you should at least stay home today and give your body more time to rest."

"Fine," he groused.

"I'll get you something to eat. Be right back."

"Arianwen?" he called out as I reached the door.

I stopped and turned to look at him. "Yes, Verus?"

He looked down, a muscle ticking in his jaw. "I'm sorry about last night . . . That was a mistake. It won't happen again."

His words pierced my heart and made it ache in a way I had not thought possible. "Which part?" I gritted out, trying to keep my voice from betraying my feelings. "The part where you stood up to the Iris, or the part where you kissed me?"

His eyes flashed to mine, and I waited for him to respond. Was I really that unloveable? Would it be so terrible to try to build a real marriage between us?

The silence was deafening until he finally cleared his throat and said, "All of it."

"Understood." I whirled back around and fled to the kitchen.

CHAPTER 23

THE DAWNING

ARIANWEN

Returning to the sacred lagoon to attend Leilani's dawning ceremony felt strange. Surrounded by family and friends, everyone expected us to be a perfect little family, so we pretended. We had, after all, gotten fairly good at it over the past year and a half.

The large flame of the bonfire we sat around crackled, shooting sparks and embers about. Its rising heat distorted the shapes and figures dancing on the other side. I watched other couples stomp and twirl to the beat of drums, their movements in sync and their passions pure as they snuck off to partake in each other's bodies. Overwhelming feelings of dissatisfaction swept over me, a desire for something that was so clearly out of reach.

Verus sat beside me, an arm flung casually over my shoulders, but his body tensed the moment I leaned into him—yet another rejection. Was he ever going to let me in again? For a brief moment, after spending that day together weeks ago, it had been as though his tough exterior had cracked and a glimmer of hope had shone through, a sign that things might have changed between us. But then, as if it had all been a dream, he'd gone back to treating me as if I didn't exist.

I recounted our interactions, looking for clues of what I may have said or done to drive him off. Had Verus not believed me when I'd assured him that I didn't care about where we lived or the fact that he'd never be a shipwright? Was that really enough of a reason for the sudden regret and distance? The wealth, the lifestyle, meant nothing to me, surely he could see that. But his continued rejection hurt, and I wasn't sure if it was worth trying again after all the disappointment.

Verus left my side and wandered over to the tables set up with food. My stomach grumbled—as though it too shared the empty pit of dissatisfaction that had taken hold of me—but I couldn't bring myself to follow him. I stayed with our daughter while she played and dug for shells in the glowing sand. The night would carry on, and just as the tide would rise and then fall, I'd sit here on my own, watching the dancers dance.

My sister was glowing in the starlight, absolutely radiant. She had her arms around a young Argenti male who looked at her as if she'd hung the stars in the sky. I was happy she had found love, if not a tiny bit jealous. Okay, I was a lot jealous . . . but I was also genuinely happy for her. My parents seemed willing to arrange the match as well, making her one very lucky Argenti. Though part of me knew she'd get her way even if they hadn't initially agreed. Being the youngest daughter, she had that effect on my father.

My eyes wandered back toward the sprawling buffet of food, but Verus was nowhere in sight. Curiosity mixed with hunger motivated me to get up. Now was my chance to get something to eat.

"Mother, would you keep an eye on Aella, please?" I asked.

"Of course, darling," she replied. "Go have fun."

"Thank you," I murmured softly before making my way to the tables.

As usual, my parents had provided a lovely spread of fruits and pastries, and my mouth watered at the roasted fish. I grabbed a skewer and let myself feast on the sight of friends and lovers as they danced wild and free, guided by nothing but source and starlight. Perhaps I would join them. It had been far too long since I'd let go and let the music take me away from my troubles.

The deep timbre of Verus' voice filtered through the trees scattered along the beach, piquing my interest. I looked over and spotted him with his parents standing off to the side. They didn't look pleased, and I rolled my eyes, hoping they weren't giving him a hard time about his work situation. I had honestly hoped they wouldn't come. Even with Verus' insistence to raise Aella as his own child, they held it over me like a bane, continuously making their displeasure clear as though I could possibly forget. The less we saw of them, the better, in my opinion.

Absolutely no good would come from listening in on their conversation.

You know better, Ari. Walk away. Now.

But the chances of Verus telling me about it was zero, so against all my better judgment, I nonchalantly made my way closer to them, doing my best to stay out of their lines of sight.

"This is all her fault. Her unfaithfulness to you before the wedding is more than enough cause to have your marriage annulled."

My fault? The absurdity of her words clanged in my head.

"You and Father both knew full well the terms to which you agreed upon her return," Verus replied. "Just because things didn't work out the way you wanted them to doesn't give you the right to suddenly play the victim."

"But it's true! She ruined you, Verus! Can't you see? The child's father doesn't even want anything to do with that cursed female. Why do you think that is? You can't trust her. She's a scourge on your life," she spat out. "The Iris will know what to do with her. You don't need to worry about her anymore. We traveled here to ask you to come home. We can easily find you a new wife back in the Westhen Isles. In fact, there is this lovely girl who would be perfect for you."

I bit my tongue to keep myself from butting in. As crazy as it sounded, I wasn't surprised they were trying to blame me for Verus' altercation with the Iris. They'd never seen me as more than a way to advance in life anyway, so it only made sense they would blame this on me. But Verus had always stood up for me and Aella, regardless of his guarded nature. I had no doubt in my mind he would continue to do so. He would never take his mother's hateful accusations seriously. But as I waited and waited for his certain rebuttal, the silence stretched impossibly long, my confidence fading with every breath.

"Verus, you know your mother is right. We should have never agreed to this marriage to begin with. There's still time to start over. What do you say?"

I held my breath.

"I'll consider it," he replied.

The world stopped, my breath trapped in my lungs.

What?

He'll consider it?

The feeling of betrayal cut so deep, it felt like choking just to breathe, my throat full of glass. The cords of my dress became like a vise around my chest, squeezing tighter and tighter, the corners of my vision going dark around me, threatening to close in.

I guess I had my answer. Our marriage truly was over.

A sob burst from my lips as reality came crashing in.

Verus turned, and his eyes captured mine, widening in surprise as he saw me slowly backing away. I twisted and ran into the thick copse of trees to my left, away from the dancers and the light of the fires. I had to get away. I couldn't face him. I couldn't believe that I was being tossed aside so easily yet again. My past was repeating itself, and there was nothing I could do to stop it. I wasn't enough. I would never be enough.

My heart cracked, my tears blurring my vision as I stumbled through the sand. I thought I heard the echoes of my name breaking though the storm of anguish brewing inside, being called from behind me, but no, I had to be imagining it.

Finally, I stopped, reaching my hand out to steady myself on a tree, my shoulders heaving with sobs.

It was too much.

I couldn't continue like this.

It was never supposed to be like this.

"Arianwen."

CHAPTER 24

TO LIVE WITHOUT LOVE

VERUS

She looked so small holding herself up against the tree, but at the sound of my voice, she straightened. It was as if she were steeling herself for battle. How had we gotten here?

"Haven't you hurt me enough? I don't want to do this right now."

"What did you hear?" I asked, though I knew she'd heard enough.

She turned, tearstained eyes flashing with anger and pain. "What did I hear?" She held up both hands. "Just tell me now: when are you kicking us out? Will you even give me a chance to run before you turn me over to the Iris? I thought . . . I had hoped . . ." Her voice cracked, and I felt something breaking inside even as anger roiled through me.

"Isn't this what you wanted?" I spat. "I know what you've been planning. You were going to take Aella and leave *me*. Why shouldn't I consider my parents' request?"

"What?" Her jaw dropped. "What in the stars are you talking about, Verus? I don't want to go anywhere. This is my home."

"I heard you talking to that male near the hospitium about getting out of Iveria."

"What are you—" She paused, and a light of understanding filled her eyes as she shook her head. "I can explain that—it's not what you think. I needed to have a plan to get out of Iveria in case our family was ever in danger . . ."

I couldn't help but scoff. "And you didn't think to let me in on those plans? You thought you could just take her away without telling me . . .?"

"I don't know. Maybe if you stopped pushing me away all the time, I wouldn't have to make plans all on my own. Because, let's face it, Verus, the two of us have been living completely separate lives. It's pretty hard to make plans with someone who won't even speak with me. We may have had one good day together, but how was I to know if that would last? And I wanted a plan in case something else happened with the Iris—we haven't exactly made the safest choices where they're concerned!" she blurted, her face flushed red.

"I don't know what you want from me, Arianwen. I live with the gravity of my mistake every day. Do you know how much it kills me that I will never be able to give you the life you were used to? I feel responsible to provide for you and keep you safe, and the idea that you felt compelled to look for safety elsewhere makes me wonder if you actually meant what you said about being okay with a life beneath . . ."

"I am! I meant every word I said to you," she said. "Why didn't you just ask me about what you overheard?"

I stared at her, clenching my jaw, my pride keeping me from responding. I *wanted* to believe that she didn't care about living a humble life, but the shame of not being able to give her what I'd promised was overwhelming.

"I'm sorry, Verus. I should have told you about my plans."

I gave her a stiff nod in acknowledgement.

"I can't explain *everything*, but Lucris is the leader of a rebellion here, and I've been trying to help where I can. The Iris, they—" She winced.

My heart stuttered in my chest, and once again, I was angry at the unnamed male who had made her swear that damned oath.

"I don't even know what to say," I gritted out.

"Are you ever going to let me in? Tell me what you're actually thinking?"

she asked, tears welling in her eyes again. "Maybe I *should* leave if this is what our future holds. I'm so tired of pretending to be this happy family in front of our loved ones only to go home and continue on our separate ways."

"We had an agreement," I said, clenching my fists.

"Maybe at first . . . but I was starting to think that maybe you cared a little?" She looked up at me, her cheeks wet with tears. "You do things for me, for us, that make me think you might care, but then you disappear and you rarely talk to me . . . You are a wonderful father to Aella, and I will never deny that. But for all of your kindness, I feel as if I am a ghost in our home. You only show me affection when we are around other people, but even then, I feel you holding back. Sometimes, you give me small glimpses of what our life could be like . . . but then you take it all back, call it a mistake."

"I can never give you what you want, Arianwen! Even if I wanted to, I do not have a whole heart to give you, and—"

"I have tried to show you who I am, and with the exception of a few months of my life, I will tell you whatever you want to know," she interrupted. "But you? You're a stranger. Every time I try to get closer to you, you lock me out. What are you so stars-damned afraid of?"

"I'm not afraid of anything," I growled.

"Prove it, Verus. Show me who you are. I can't bear to live the rest of my life with a stranger— I might as well be alone."

"Is that what you want? Would you rather be alone?"

"No! I want you to let me in. I want you to give this marriage a real chance," she begged.

"It will only hurt you."

"I've heard that one before. Try me. Do you think you are the only one who understands pain?"

I shook my head. "No, I don't, but—"

"What is so terrible, Verus? What are you so afraid to tell me?"

She tilted her chin up as if preparing herself, and I hesitated. I knew she'd been hurt before, and the last thing I wanted was to cause her any more pain. I couldn't stand the fact that I'd been hurting her so much with my distance.

I took a deep, shuddering breath, and before I could take them back, the words tumbled out of my mouth. "Her name is Lyani." *Is*, not was. A part of me had to believe she was still alive, even if we'd never see each other again.

She took a step back, her eyes wide. "You're in love with someone else? You're *with* someone else?"

"It's not like that," I said vehemently. "I have not betrayed our marriage vows, no matter what you might think. Not once."

She crossed her arms, gripping her elbows as she processed my words. "What happened?"

"Before you and I were betrothed, I fell in love with a girl—Lyani. I'm fairly certain she is my true mate, the one the stars destined for me. Except, my parents did not approve. They insisted I marry above my station to help our family, and because I was working with your father, they were able to arrange our marriage."

She nodded for me to continue, and I was surprised how easily the words came now that I had opened up.

"The biggest irony is that everyone gave you such a hard time for running away, when, all along, I'd made plans to do the same. I'd asked Lyani to run away from Iveria, to make our own path together, but she refused to leave her family. I begged and begged her to go, especially with the second draft coming up, but still, she kept refusing . . . She loved Iveria, she couldn't bring herself to give it up . . . and I couldn't make her, no matter how hard I tried. And then . . . she was chosen."

Arianwen gasped, a hand going to her heart.

I took a breath, squeezing my eyes shut as the memories flooded my mind. "I had to watch my mate leave for Prisma, knowing I would never see her again, never hear from her again. I'll never know if she won or if she is serving in some Iris household. The entire future I had planned for myself, gone. My heart boarded that ship, and I swore I'd never love another."

"Verus." Her voice cracked, and I looked up, meeting her gaze.

"So even after the scandal of your disappearance, marrying you, the stars couldn't have planned it better. You clearly wanted as little from the marriage as I did, and you had a child on the way, so we'd be able to fulfill the expectations placed on us by the Iris. It seems perfect. We can both live our separate lives with no expectation from each other."

"What are you trying to say?"

"Perhaps we can both have what we wanted . . . You seem content with your work. Why can't we just remain as we are?"

"That might have worked in the beginning, Verus, but can you really live without love for the rest of your existence?"

I flinched, looking down at the sand. "I can never give you what you deserve, Arianwen. My heart was never mine to give. She took it with her when she left."

Even as the words left my mouth, I could hear the lie I was afraid to voice. While Lyani *had* taken my heart with her, from the moment Arianwen had walked toward me on the beach, I'd felt something stirring within. As much as I'd tried to fight it, I cared for her in a way I'd never thought would have been possible again.

I looked up, and the expression on her face nearly broke me once more. She was owed the truth—I owed it to myself to come clean. "Maybe you're right. I am afraid . . . I'm afraid that the broken and shattered pieces of my heart will never be enough for you . . . I'm afraid that if I do let you in, you'll leave too, that the one you left behind will come and take both of you away."

Her face filled with shock and understanding. With a watery smile, she held up her palm, letting the starlight hit the mark seared into her skin. "I may not be able to speak of what happened to me during those months, but I lost a part of my heart too. That is why I was willing to go along with your plan. I needed time to grieve, time to heal . . . but holding on to the past, holding on to our pain, it's not going to bring them back."

Our eyes held each other, a mutual understanding passing between us.

A soft laugh fell from her lips. "What if we're actually perfect for each other? Two wounded and fragmented souls. The stars tried to break us, but what if we prove them wrong?"

I reached over, swiping a tear off her face gently with my thumb. "Maybe you're right . . . and perhaps we should try."

"That's all I ask," she said, smiling as I cupped her cheek.

"I can't promise that I'll change overnight, Arianwen."

"That's okay. I understand."

"Maybe we can start over?" I asked.

"Start over how?"

"Try to get to know each other, holding nothing back."

"I'd honestly love that, Verus."

"I'll do my best."

"Well, I'll go first." She stuck out her hand. "Hello, I'm Arianwen, your wife. I love adventure, healing is my calling, and I enjoy long swims along the beach."

I let out a small chuckle and gripped her hand in mine. "Nice to meet you, *wife*. I'm Verus, your husband, and I enjoy cooking, cliff-diving, and I'd kill for chocolate cake."

"Chocolate cake?" she said with a laugh. "I've never seen you eat chocolate cake."

"Well, I said I like to cook, not that I can bake . . . and based on experience, I wasn't about to ask you to make me one," I teased her.

She rolled her eyes, her face flushing. "One time, Verus. I burned the pastries one time."

"You only made pastries *one time*," I teased.

"You're never going to let me live that one down, are you?" she asked with a smile before taking a deep, shuddering breath, looking as if she was finally free of a heavy burden. Admittedly, I felt lighter too.

"Faex, we've been gone for a while. I can only imagine what our families must be thinking," she said, looking around nervously.

Without even thinking, I reached over, mussing her hair. "Oh, we can give them something to talk about."

She playfully smacked my chest. "Verus, our parents are out there."

"All the better," I teased before pushing her up against the tree, leaning my forehead against hers, our sudden proximity causing all the blood in my body to rush south.

"What are you doing?" she asked breathlessly.

"There's only one thing missing to make this ruse complete . . ." I murmured, my eyes dropping to her lips. Ever since that kiss the other night, I'd been longing to taste her again.

"Oh?" Her tongue darted out, wetting her lips as she stared up at me, tugging at those pieces of my heart I thought I'd never get back.

I leaned in closer. "Your lips . . . They don't look swollen from kissing."

"Well, that just won't do," she whispered softly, tilting her face up in offering.

Very tentatively, I lowered my mouth to hers and kissed her. She opened for me the moment my tongue teased the seam of her lips, and it was like coming home. She tasted like honeyed wine, her lavender scent winding its way up my nose. I pulled her bottom lip into my mouth, gently biting down, loving the gasp that came out of her. I'd have bottled that sound if I could have. Before I could pin her to the tree and take this further, I pulled away, my breath coming in short, uneven bursts.

"I hope that was all right," I said, feeling oddly shy. "Now you look properly ravished."

I needed more. That kiss awakened something in me, and now that the walls between us had been knocked down, I wanted to give her all of me. I wanted all of her.

Blushing, she smiled before stepping around me. "We should probably head back."

She made it two steps before I grabbed her arm, pulling her back into me, my lips capturing hers in another breath-stealing kiss. I dug my free hand into her hair at the nape of her neck, pulling her closer, our kiss a clash of tongues and teeth, filled with pent-up passion and longing.

I dropped her arm, hitching my hand around her thigh, pulling our bodies flush as I ground into her, needing to feel her warmth.

"Verus," she gasped, followed by a whimper as I started kissing my way down her neck, my hand sliding around her throat before trailing down her chest.

She set me on fire, every inch ablaze with need as I returned to her lips and consumed the beautiful female who clung to me and kissed me as if I were all she'd ever need.

We were broken and healing, but we belonged to each other.

As she dug her hands into my hair, I shuddered as the sensation of her hands and her lips threatened to take me to a place of no return. Every suppressed desire came raging to the surface, and I wanted to take her right there on the beach.

She rocked her hips into me, and I groaned, "I will have you right here, right now, if you keep that up, wife."

"You read my mind." She chuckled, pulling back slightly to look into my eyes.

"As delightful as that sounds," I mused, "I'd rather not worry about one of your siblings coming over here looking for you."

She shivered at the thought. "That's probably for the best, husband . . ."

I let go of her thigh, and we stepped apart. Blowing out a breath, a hesitant smile turned up my lips. "I hope that wasn't moving too quickly . . ."

"I think it was pretty clear I was enjoying myself," she teased.

"I can't believe it took me that long to properly kiss you. One kiss just wasn't enough." I pulled her back into my arms, resting my head on top of hers. "I'm glad we talked . . . and while I don't know if my heart will ever truly feel whole again, every broken and shattered part that remains is yours if you will have me."

"Always and forever, Verus . . ." she whispered softly.

She leaned into me, and I loved how she fit perfectly in my arms, her body molded to mine. I almost couldn't believe that this was real, that I was holding her, that she would stay.

"Let's go home, wife," I said finally, tucking her into my side as we walked toward a new future . . . together.

CHAPTER 25
Broken Parts and All

ARIANWEN

Verus laid a sleeping Aella gently in her cot. He truly was a wonderful father. Even if he thought he had no heart left to give, I knew the truth. He had opened it to our daughter, and he loved her, and I knew we'd find a depth of love for each other too.

Verus stood watch over her, softly lulling her back to sleep with one of the old lullabies. My heart almost burst in my chest. *What now?* I was overflowing with emotions after everything that had been said and that kiss. I pressed two fingers to my lips as I remembered the sensation, the taste of him.

He turned toward me, raising a brow in question. My eyes were shimmering with unshed tears, and I took a step toward him but faltered.

Do we pick up where we left off at the lagoon? Do I just say good night?

Stepping out into the hall, I paced back and forth, wringing my hands. Why was I so nervous?

Verus stepped out of my room and gently closed the door behind himself.

"I'm, uh, going to wash up," I said awkwardly and quickly shut myself in the bathing room. Splashing cool water on my face did nothing to calm the nerves.

What is wrong with you, Ari? You were just kissing him earlier. Why the sudden cold feet?

Gathering all my courage, I opened the door and looked out. His bedroom light was on, visible through the cracked door, so he must have been getting ready for bed. Before I lost my nerve, I quickly walked toward his room.

Verus was still humming the song he had been singing over Aella, and I smiled. The deep timbre of his voice was like a purr, the way the notes traveled across the space wrapping me up in its melody. His musical ability had been a surprising discovery the first time he'd sung Aella to sleep.

Feeling bold, I pushed the door open and entered his room, watching as he lit the lamps near the bed. He had stripped off his clothes and stood only in gray undershorts that left far too little to the imagination.

Stars, he was such a fine specimen of a male, his entire body sculpted to perfection. My fingers itched to run along the muscles of his back that lengthened and rippled as he stretched his arms overhead. I ached for him in a way I hadn't realized was possible—to feel his hands, strong and calloused, on my skin.

"Well, are you going to say something, or just stand there ogling me all night, wife?" Verus said huskily over his shoulder.

Heat flushed my face, realizing my silent perusal of his body had not gone unnoticed. "Husband . . ."

He finally turned all the way around, and it took all my self-control not to look down his body and see if my presence was affecting him as much as his was affecting me. I swallowed, unsure of what to say. Perhaps words were not what I needed. Perhaps what I needed was to stop being afraid and to act.

I crossed the divide between us, stretching up onto my tiptoes and wrapping my arms around his neck, crashing my lips into his and pulling our bodies flush against each other. He crushed me in his arms, his mouth working against mine, his tongue gently probing until I opened for him. My hands fell from around his neck to his chest, my fingers exploring every inch as he kissed me with passion and fervor.

His hands slid down my side to my thighs. He picked me up, and I quickly wrapped my legs around his waist. I moaned as the hard length of him pressed up against me. It was as if I had been living in a desert and he was the water to quench my thirst. He kissed me deeper, and I responded in kind. He was mine, and I was his, and we needed to be one.

Finally breaking apart, he rested his forehead against mine as our chests heaved, trying to catch our breaths from our marathon kiss.

Feeling suddenly shy again, I asked, "Is this moving too fast? Do we want to take things slower?"

"Arianwen." He rolled his hips into me, and I barely held back a moan. "Does it feel like I want to take this slower? I have been wanting to take you to my bed for months. It's been torturous living here with you, wanting to know if you taste just as good as I imagine."

I shuddered in his arms, heat pooling low, and I ached, longing to remove all the barriers between us. "Put me down, Verus," I said breathily.

A flash of disappointment crossed his face as he gently placed me onto my feet. I stepped back and grabbed the hem of my dress, pulling it over my head, leaving me bare except for the thin undergarment that covered my lower half.

Verus' eyes widened in surprise and delight as he hungrily took in my almost-naked form.

"Well? Are you going to stop *ogling* and have your wicked way with me?" I asked, feeling shy again at his open perusal.

Verus pulled me back into his arms with a groan, his hands deliciously rough against my soft, sensitive skin. He pressed kisses onto my neck and chest, his hands sliding up to cup my breasts, his thumbs circling the sensitive buds. I cried out as he sank his teeth into my neck, marking me, claiming me.

"I have dreamed of touching you, wife . . . "

I whimpered as he pinched me before soothing the hurt with a soft caress.

"Then touch me, husband," I gasped out as he lowered his mouth to my other breast.

"These," he growled. "I've been *dreaming* of playing with these."

A slight laugh came out of me, and I dug my nails into his back as he licked and nipped at them.

I tried pushing him back toward the bed, but it was like trying to move a tree, his body firm and unyielding.

"Would you like something, darling wife?" Verus asked as he slid his hand down my side, his fingers blazing a trail of heat as he neared where I really wanted him.

"Yes, husband. I would like you to take me to bed." I panted as he slipped his fingers beneath the hem of my undergarment.

"You feel incredible," he purred.

Without warning, he picked me up and gently threw me onto his bed.

I watched as he prowled toward me and stopped at the edge. Sliding his undershorts down, my eyes widened in surprise as the full length of him was finally revealed. *Stars, I hope he fits.* It had been too long, and I started to ache at the thought of him filling me, the desire for him building. Biting my lip, I beckoned him closer.

A feral smile lit up his face as he crawled toward me on the bed. He slid my undergarment down my legs and discarded it on the floor, then grabbed one leg and started kissing his way up it. Before he got too close to my center, he moved to the other leg, showing it just as much care and attention.

I writhed impatiently on the bed, my need for him burning within me.

Verus stopped, gripping my legs tightly as he looked up at me from between them. "I've changed my mind, Arianwen . . ."

"What?" I almost squeaked.

A smirk twisted his lips before he continued. "About taking things slow. I've longed to taste you for what feels like forever, and I intend to enjoy every drawn-out second of this."

I threw my head back as he started working me with his lips, tongue, and fingers.

Heat continued building in my core as he brought me closer and closer to my breaking point, and I cried out as waves of pleasure rushed over me.

"That's my beautiful wife," he praised as he kissed his way up my body after I'd finished.

"Verus . . ."

"Keep saying my name in that breathy way, and this will continue all night long," he purred into my ear before nipping at it.

"Is that a promise?" I asked, my lips turning up into a contented smile, admiring his toned biceps as he held himself up over me with one arm.

"I promise that you will never be left wanting when I'm around," he said before his purposeful touch caused me to cry out and arch up against him.

I slid my hand down his taut abdomen, gripping him tightly, enjoying his sudden gasp and how his muscles tensed against me.

"You've been neglected, dear husband."

He smiled down at me, then suddenly furrowed his brow. "Do you have any tonic?" he asked. "Let's not have any surprises until we are ready for them."

His thoughtfulness thrilled me. "Yes, husband. I can whip some up."

"Thank the stars," he groaned as he pushed into me.

He filled me completely, almost to the point of discomfort, but as our bodies moved together, the warmth built and built. My legs wrapped around his waist, allowing him in deeper. He kissed me thoroughly, passionately. I gripped his chiseled arms, loving the strength and power he exuded as he utterly wrecked my body and made me his.

He gently turned me onto my stomach and lifted my hips, the new angle causing me to cry out all over again. Wrapping his hands around the front of me, he drew me up toward him so that my back was flush against his chest, and he kissed my neck and shoulder.

I started tensing around him again, my release within reach.

"Verus, I'm so close . . ." I moaned.

"That's it, my lovely wife . . . Come for me again," he whispered into my ear.

This time, he let himself go too and roared his release as our bodies shuddered and pulsed together.

Collapsing onto the bed, he wrapped his giant arms around me, pushing one of his legs between mine. We fit perfectly. Perhaps Verus and I were two broken halves that could become something new together . . . something better than what we could have been apart.

"That was . . . incredible," I breathed.

Verus shook the bed with his full-bodied laugh. "That's putting it lightly. *You* are incredible, my wife. I can't believe you were able to resist me for so long."

I reached back and gently pinched his side. "Watch that smart mouth, or I'll make you wait again."

"You wouldn't dare . . . You enjoyed yourself far too much. I have the marks to prove it."

I chuckled. "You're probably right." A contented sigh came out of me, and I turned in his arms so I could see his face. "I want you to know that I have no intention of leaving, as long as you'll have me."

Surprise flashed over his features before his lips tugged into a smile. "Then I guess we're stuck together, because you're not getting rid of me, broken parts and all . . . I choose you, Arianwen."

With those words, a torn part of my heart started to mend, and I began to feel whole again.

CHAPTER 26
A New Side of Verus

ARIANWEN

The next morning, as I was preparing breakfast for us, Verus came up behind me and wrapped his arms around my middle, giving me a sweet peck on the cheek.

"Good morning, wife. I trust that the little rest you got was restorative."

I huffed a laugh as I did my best not to get distracted and burn the food. Aella cooed from her highchair, and Verus left my side to kiss the top of her head.

"How is my sweet girl?"

My heart melted all over again. Verus truly was such a doting father.

Putting our breakfast on plates, I carried them over to the table and took a seat as Verus prepared some strong tea for us. When he finally joined me, pulling his chair as close to mine as possible, I looked down at my plate as a sudden timidity came over me.

"Come now, my darling wife. We spent the entire evening together naked. Why are you shy now?"

His brashness had me laughing as I looked up and met his gaze. "This is a new side to you, Verus. One I did not expect."

"I expect you to learn all my sides, Arianwen." He winked suggestively.

I couldn't stop the blush that flooded my cheeks. "Shh! Our daughter is listening."

Verus turned and smiled at her. "Don't worry. She won't remember any of this. If anything, I hope she always knows how very much I adore you . . . even if it grosses her out eventually."

"If you say so." I grinned. "Well . . . now that things have changed between us, what does that mean for our future? We briefly mentioned the tonic last night, but what about moving forward? I'm sure you want children of your own."

His eyes darkened briefly. "Aella *is* my own. She's my heart. If she is the only child we ever have, she is more than enough."

"You are the best father, Verus, and I adore you for saying that, but do you want more?"

"I would love to have more children when you are ready, but I know you have dreams too. I want you to be able to pursue them, and having more children right now would make that difficult."

I sat back in my seat in surprise, sudden tears welling in my eyes. "Do you truly mean that?"

"I will never lie to you, Arianwen. Of course I mean it. I want you to complete your healing studies and apprenticeship. You deserve more than what you have now. You could be running an entire hospitium—that is how much I believe in you."

"That means the world to me, Verus. Thank you for understanding."

"I have some extra coin saved that we can use for childcare, and perhaps our families can help with Aella as well. Now that she's getting older, she doesn't need to be attached to you at all times."

"I don't know . . . I worry about someone else watching her and perhaps realizing she . . ." I couldn't even finish my sentence. How did Verus rationalize her air element? Perhaps he just thought she was blessed by the stars, the mark on her neck proof of that. The weight of her parentage hung heavy over me, and not being able to share it with him was painful, but it was not as if we could speak of such things. As much as it hurt, it would be safer for everyone if no one ever found out.

Verus grabbed my hand and squeezed it. "It's okay to learn how to let go. Aella will be perfectly safe, and we won't let anything happen to her. I promise."

He leaned in and captured my lips with his. The kiss was gentle and sweet, full of promise. I slid out of my seat and into his lap, wrapping my arms around his neck, letting him kiss and soothe away all my worries and concerns.

Before it could turn into heated passion, I untangled myself from his arms and went to clean up the mess Aella had made. I'd have loved nothing more than to spend the rest of the day exploring his body and finding out what else his tongue was capable of, but we had a daughter and responsibilities to think of.

Faex. My mind drifted back to that thing he'd done with my arms up over my head . . .

"Arianwen."

"Yes, Verus?"

"Stop thinking about last night before we traumatize our daughter and I take you right here on the table in front of her."

I blushed furiously and hurried out of the room, Aella giggling the entire way.

EPILOGUE

ARIANWEN

Aella splashed in the shallow water of the cove as Verus and I watched the sky melt from blue to crimson with the setting of the sun. Our fingers were intertwined, resting on the silky, pink sand.

"I love this spot," I said, my lips curled up in a smile.

"It's pretty nice," Verus agreed.

"Promise me that no matter how busy our lives get, we will always make time to return to this place and just be."

Verus chuckled, pulling my hand up to his mouth and placing a soft kiss on the back of it. "As you wish, my beautiful wife."

Aella yawned and blinked her eyes, letting out a soft cry.

"Ah, yes. It's time to head home and get our little whirlwind to bed," Verus said, looking at our daughter with such love that I couldn't help but smile.

"I can't wait to get home," I replied, my heart warming with the realization that I truly meant it. No longer did it make me feel alone—it was a place filled with joy and laughter.

I jumped to my feet, grabbing the bag with our things and slinging it over my shoulder. As I stepped toward Aella, I found myself tripping over a piece of driftwood I hadn't noticed sticking out of the sand. Strong arms surrounded me, catching me before I hit the ground.

"I've got you, Arianwen."

If you enjoyed this book, please leave us a review!
Join us for the epic conclusion of
The Stars Would Curse Us Series with
The Stars Could Save Us
Coming November 2024

Acknowledgements

First and foremost, we would like to thank God for the gifts of creativity and storytelling, and our families for all of their love, patience, and encouragement.

Justin, thank you for your unwavering support and positivity. Every time I wanted to quit, your belief in me kept me going. Thanks for helping me block out scenes. IYKYK.

To Oren, my strongest advocate, you always brag about me and force me to get out there and talk about my book when my instincts would have me pretending I'm not a real author. Your commitment to not hearing any spoilers always brings a smile, knowing you love the story that much.

To our children, whose adorable questions about the book make us smile. (No, you're not allowed to read this anytime soon.)

Holly and Suz, alpha readers extraordinaire, it's always amazing how each draft of a book changes and grows. Thank you for being the first to read this story and help it reach its fullest potential. (P.S. Thanks, Suz, for Papa Goose.)

Rachel, the best developmental/copy/line/proofer in the biz. Honestly, we can't imagine working with anyone else. You're one of our biggest cheerleaders, and a dear friend. Thank you for sharpening and honing our writing to make it shine, and for your endless hours and patience with us.

To the Dinner Roll Population, you know who you are and what you did.

Our incredible Beta Team: Jaclyn McMillan, Karrie W., KL Hester, Laura F., M.A. Brown, and Sierra, thank you! Our book wouldn't be where it is without all of your incredibly thoughtful feedback. Thank you for hyping us up with all the love and unhinged comments.

Much gratitude to our MTP family for loving on us. We are so grateful for the friendships we've developed over the past year and appreciate all of the guidance and support.

To our brand new baby street team, thank you for believing in us and helping us spread the word about this series. Every post and share gets our books in front of a wider audience and we can't thank you enough.

Finally, to our readers, thank you for coming on this journey with us, and for falling in love with these characters. We do this for you. Thank you for the unhinged DMs, the beautiful social media posts, and sharing your love of books.

About the Authors

Meet Stephanie Combs and Valerie Rivers, a dynamic sister duo who share an enthusiasm for writing and storytelling.

Stephanie's passion for literature ignited at a young age, shaping her into an insatiable reader. Her love for writing began with crafting short fictional tales and poetry during her childhood—a spark that only intensified as she delved into writing stories for her college newspaper while pursuing a degree in Broadcast Journalism. Stephanie's sense of humor shines through her writing, infusing her work with witty banter and endearing characters. She resides in Maryland with her musical husband and four rambunctious children. When she's not sneaking in a writing session, you can find her nose stuck in a book or baking goodies for the family.

Valerie resides in sunny South Florida with her pilot husband and three children. Not your typical fantasy author, she brings a fresh perspective to the genre due to her unique background as an artist and intensive care nurse. In her free time, when she isn't writing, she's either working on her next art project obsession or lost in the landscape of her imagination. Embracing her inherent creativity, she weaves fantasy worlds and crafts captivating narratives that transport readers to breathtaking realms of wonder.

You can find more on their website at:
silverflamebooks.com

Follow them on Instagram:
Stephanie - @stephdevourerofbooks
Valerie - @valerieriversauthor

More From Stephanie & Valerie

The Stars Would Curse Us Series

The Stars Would Curse Us (Book 1)
The Stars Couldn't Break Us (Book 1.5)
The Stars Could Save Us (Book 2) (Nov '24)

More From Midnight Tide

The Songs That Beckon by M.A. Brown

Their grief binds them
The Song calls them
The Darkness wants to claim them

As winter wraps Areth in its frozen embrace, nightmarish beasts descend upon the Hastings household kidnapping Mr. and Mrs. Hastings and leaving behind their daughter, Bianca, as sole witness. In the wake of their abduction her quiet world is turned upside down and shaken revealing the secrets and lies her parents have buried.

As truths unravel it binds her to those who have similarly lost. Together they must wade through the thorny tangles of growing love and grief to find those that they hold dear before the looming threat of darkness is unleashed to destroy them all.

Travel worlds in this dark, dreamy and romantic debut filled with dusty books and pining looks.

Available Now

www.ingramcontent.com/pod-product-compliance
Lightning Source LLC
Chambersburg PA
CBHW021709190726
48289CB00008B/2439